Rivets and Revolution

By Jessica Lucci

Rivets and Revolution

By Jessica Lucci

ISBN: 978-1-7323495-7-5

To the Waltham Museum and Waltham Historical Society, for bringing history to life.

Ense petit placidam sub libertate quietum.

By the sword we seek peace, but peace only under liberty.

Chapter 1

"We are getting too old for this."

"Speak for yourself!"

Georgia and Liberty skated on their mechanical boots, balancing on the thin silver blades that cut through the layer of ice covering the streets of Boston. As the blades spun forward, the two women sashayed, stretching their legs expertly.

They had started at the Charles River, between their two homes, between the delineation of the Crown and the Patriots. Then, with flushed, cold faces and bright eyes squinting into the glare of spring's last snow, they dallied hand in hand. The blades slowly drove them forward. A small crowd had gathered before them. Angry shouts carried clearly on the calm, frosty air.

"Disperse, Doodles!" The laughing British soldier was brave upon his trusted steed. The size of a shed, with the shine of metal, the unicorn's long, pointed head sword flashed in a random ribbon of sunlight.

"Lobsters! Crawl back to the sea, where you belong!" Liberty shouted.

Georgia grabbed her lover's arm. "Liberty, I think we should leave here."

Liberty's eyes narrowed as she stared into the crowd. She could feel the heat of indignation rise up her neck. She wore pants because her old mentor had taught her safety was a top priority, and long skirts could easily be snatched in the gears and rollers of the printing press. Dresses were not in her common wear. Besides, pants were more useful when climbing the tree to Georgia's bedroom. And it was much quicker to redress after one of their trysts. After a lifetime of wearing clothing suitable for a male, Liberty felt comfortable in that attire. The townspeople overlooked her eccentricity in this manner because they respected her so well.

She didn't socialize much, but everyone knew her because Liberty was the one with news. Her investigative mind scanned the faces in the growing mob of British soldiers and ordinary colonists expressing their rage over totalitarian rule.

Georgia's worried voice snapped Liberty back into crazy, cold reality. "Stop, please."

They had reached King Street, by the Custom House. Liberty usually veered away from this heavily occupied spot, but with Georgia, she welcomed some light adventure.

As the taunts grew louder, though, Liberty could not resist skating forward to see better.

"Isn't that Henry Knox?" Liberty recognized the bookseller who frequented her printing press, where she was Master Printer.

"Insolent insurrectionists! Disperse at once, or else feel the mighty hand of your superiors!"

Georgia tugged at Liberty's glove. "No, we must not involve ourselves. It is none of our business."

Liberty held fast to her leather-gloved hand but stopped pulling. "Of course it is our business! This is our homeland, and it is our duty to stay informed."

"Off with you and your curiosity then. I am staying put." Georgia leaned back, away from the commotion.

"Really? You don't want to see what all the hubbub is about?"

Georgia looked with worry at the loud group. Then her blue eyes met Liberty's brown ones. "I have a feeling I will soon read all about it. Go on, I'll wait here."

"I'll be right back."

Liberty gracefully slid toward the angry mob. The British had raised their weapons: automatic slingshots, like mini-trebuchets. No doubt stolen from the French. Liberty scowled.

The British troops and Patriots slung insults back and forth. While the taunting rapidly increased into incoherent shouts, Liberty slid towards the invisible partition between the two raging sides.

"Mongrels, go back to your kennels! Disperse!" the soldier on the mecha-horse shouted.

"Says who?" replied a deep voice from the crowd.

"Says the Crown!"

Liberty reached between her skates and with her red woolen mittens, scooped up a ball of slushy snow. "To the crown!" She lunged back and threw the snowball with as much power as she could muster on her spinning blades. It knocked the hat right off the loudest soldier's head.

Other colonists soon followed suit, covering the soldiers' red uniforms with grey wetness.

The commanding officer on the mecha-horse called, "Launch!"

The line of soldiers reached into their long, deep satchels and loaded their mini-trebuchets. Within seconds, fist-sized rubber bullets bought from southern traders zipped into the crowd. Cries of pain mixed with wicked laughter. "Go fetch, dogs!"

Liberty formed another snowball. It had just left the sopping cloth of her gloves when she saw it, in slow motion, yet she didn't have time to move. The thick rubber bullet hit her in the middle of her forehead, and down she fell. The crowd was rioting, but beyond the melee, she could hear a woman screaming. Probably Georgia.

Liberty tried to lift herself from the cold, icy street, but legs and stomping feet were everywhere around her.

A brown hand reached down and grabbed her tightly under one armpit. Liberty struggled to get up and soon found herself in the arms of a young Black man. His deep eyes were focused directly on her with concern and strength.

"My name is Crispus Attucks. The Regulars are sure to be arresting people now. We must get away while we can."

Liberty nodded her head and her vision blurred. She blinked away sticky blood.

Attucks supported her from the backs of her arms and wheeled her away from the fray with her blades spinning before them.

"Liberty!" Georgia slid into Attucks in her haste to reach them. He held his ground as she clung to him for balance.

"Ma'am, we must get away at once. There is no way either of us will survive prison."

Georgia pointed in the opposite direction, towards Dunkerhook Road, at the far end of the British-occupied city.

"That's where the Loyalists live, though." His face bore wrinkles of frustration.

"We will be fine. We just need to get to that grove."

Liberty leaned against Attucks. "Get ready to run," she whispered.

They poised, prepared for the right moment, when no one seemed to be looking. Liberty stared into the grove.

They raced across the field.

"After them!" called a voice with the timbre of authority.

Liberty felt every bump in the ground. As much as she disliked having to rely on people, she was grateful for Attucks's brave help.

"Stop!" called Liberty.

"We can't!" Georgia shot a quick look over her shoulder. "They'll catch up with us!"

"But I see something."

"Oh, Liberty," Georgia's voice cracked, "your eyes are covered with blood."

"Attucks, do you see it?" asked Liberty. "It's the size of a small pony, shaggy, with a thick wispy tail, pointed ears…"

Attucks squinted into the shade and slowed down. Georgia slowed down with him and peeked back at a lone soldier traipsing through the bare meadow.

"I see it now," said Attucks.

Georgia looked where Liberty pointed.

There in the glade was a dark shadow. Darker than the foliage around it. It lifted its head and faced them. Black eyes stared into Liberty's brown ones.

"A wolf!" squeaked Georgia.

"You there," came a deep voice behind them. "In the name of the Crown, I order you to remain and step no further."

"Listen," whispered Liberty, afraid of spooking the wolf. "Do you hear something? The sound of metal nettles clanging against each other?"

From the far end of a brush pile, a hulking figure wobbled back and forth.

Liberty breathed relief. "It's only a mecha-porcupine."

"Those things can be vicious if not programmed properly," warned Attucks.

Liberty wiped blood from her eyebrows and watched as the sheep-sized automaton shifted its quills with a series of automated pulleys and gears, using magnetic power. The wolf's hackles went up and it bared its white teeth in black gums. Its eyes moved from her to the porcupine.

The metal creature meandered on its course, effectively performing its job of deterring wolves and other live-stock killing animals.

The wolf flattened his ears, yipped at the porcupine, and circled it.

"You there, what business have you out here today?" The soldier had stopped running when he saw them pause, and was now walking at a careful pace across the icy meadow

The wolf chanced to nip at the automaton's hindquarters, which enacted the barbed tail's swinging mechanism. With a yelp, the wolf scampered out into the deep woods. The mecha-porcupine rambled on.

"Now, with haste!" said Liberty. They raced faster than ever through sticky burrs.

The three of them made it to the grove. Liberty pushed back so she could stand on her own again. The rims of her vision were dark, but she met Attuck's eyes.

"Thank you. Georgia and I will be safe from here. But you..." She recognized the risk the enslaved man had taken in saving her. "You had best take leave of us. With all blessings. May the Great Old One pass you by."

Attucks looked around at the encroaching soldiers. "And may it never see you." He dashed into the grove and disappeared.

Georgia took her lover's arm gently. "Follow me."

"Where are we going?"

Georgia was silent as she pulled Liberty along.

"No, no, if you're thinking what I think you're thinking, it is a very bad idea."

"What's wrong? It never bothered you to visit at night."

"It's not my fault there's a long-armed maple tree pointing to your bedroom window."

"And it's just begging you to climb it?"

"Not like you beg me to climb you!"

"Dirty girl!" Georgia's face flushed.

"Too proper to talk about?" Liberty chanced a glance at her beloved's face. "I do not know if your face is red from cold or modesty. But either way, I'll find a way to warm you up."

"If I wasn't so frightened for our lives, I might laugh."

"You do not need to fear for your life, my BAP."

"I keep telling you I am not a British American Princess!"

"You say so, governor's daughter."

"I'm more than that!"

"I know, to me, you are a lot more."

"Woah, Liberty, let go!" Georgia slid into a puddle. Liberty helped her up, but then she fell backward into a drift of snow. Georgia fell on top of her.

"Oof!" Liberty lost her breath.

Their lips touched.

"Now, now, Miss Priss, can't blame me for that one."

They untangled from each other and brushed off the snow. Liberty's red mittens were wet with melted snow and fresh blood.

"No wonder why we're falling, we're still wearing our skates!" Georgia pushed the lever on her boots to draw the blades in. Then she helped Liberty with hers. "My backside is wet. I have snow on my eyelashes. Let's go home, where it is warm."

"You mean me too?"

"Sure! You're my friend. Come see what it's like to come through the door."

Liberty hesitated. "I am not sure about this. Redcoats and I don't get along well."

"I'd really like to help you, but I do not know how."

Liberty held a glove already thick with blood to her still bleeding forehead. "I could use a kiss."

Georgia leaned forward, puckered her lips, then pulled away.

"No kiss?"

"It's just that you're so..."

"Yucky? I suppose my face has seen better days."

"You are a mess. And I love you." This time Georgia did kiss Liberty's blood-tinted lips.

"Thank you." Liberty's eyes focused for the first time since she had been struck. "I love you."

"So now my dear one, will you escort me home so we can get you washed up and cozied up, with a cup of tea—"

"Georgia!" Liberty spun. "You know I haven't tasted tea since the—"

"—tariffs, I know, I am sorry, darling, I forgot to consider your feelings in my little imaginary tale. We could have sipping chocolate?"

Liberty looked down at her brown leather boots, well-worn with pride. She would need to dry the blades and mechanisms well so they wouldn't rust.

Georgia held out her arms. Liberty sighed and shuffled over. Some fights were just not worth it at the time. "Please, be wary on the way to your home, and plan for tomorrow night."

"I thought we could meet tonight?"

"Sorry, but right now it is more important for me to convalesce. And you," Liberty appraised Georgia's muddy skirt and cloak, "must attend to yourself. The servants will no doubt keep such outrages as a ruined outfit a secret."

"True, Father doesn't need to know everything."

Liberty's jaw tightened. "Like about me?" She disengaged from her lover's embrace and looked towards the woods, towards her home and purpose.

Georgia placed one hand lightly on Liberty's shoulder. "Someday, I will introduce you to Father. It just never seems like the right time."

"What's worse? That I'm a Patriot? Or that I am a woman?"

"You know as well as I how my father admires the colony's functional capabilities, including the Patriots' spirit of innovation. But you must understand the pressure he is under. He cannot cast favor upon the Patriots when he is a Crown-appointed Loyalist."

"And the fact that I am a woman?"

Georgia bit her lower lip. "I can honestly say that he would approve of you, because of your talent, ingenuity, and mostly, because you are so special to me."

Liberty reached up and patted the hand on her shoulder. Then she pulled Georgia around in front of her. She pulled open Georgia's burgundy cape and wrapped her arms around Georgia's waist. Their lips touched again.

Liberty stepped back and turned towards the woods. She squeezed Georgia's hands.

"Some secrets we keep for peace. Others we keep for passion."

"Our love is worth being a secret."

"It is also worth being accepted," Liberty said.

"As long as you know I am always with you, that my love goes where you are, I will have peace."

Liberty placed her hands on either side of Georgia's face, flattening a few stray blonde curls, and kissed her on the lips. "And I am always with you, with passion."

Liberty and Georgia embraced. Liberty's gaze spread to the woods again.

"How can I help? I could hire a mecha-horse for you."

"That wouldn't raise suspicion at all. Me traipsing through the countryside on a mechanical horse. I've never even ridden a flesh horse, never mind one that functions with gears and pulleys."

"Please, at least agree to change right into clean, dry clothes and bandage your wound."

"I will."

"Promise?"

"Promise."

Each woman turned and went their separate ways. Liberty was already writing the news article in her head: *Regulars Attack Colonists*. It was her duty as keeper and master of the press to proclaim the words of truth to the community. Even if it meant she had to sacrifice a night with Georgia.

Liberty plodded along the mushy streets leading her home, to her print shop. She passed Knox's bookshop, with his gleaming copper oxen sitting on each side of the door, silent sentinels, their tails pointed up in the resting position. Mechanical copper turkeys programmed by a series of pegs and rivets patrolled the various properties from predators. Their shiny feathers, formed like most mechanical machinations from Paul Revere's special rolled copper, shook in the slightest breeze and had the intended purpose of scaring wildlife, although flesh horses would often rear with fear upon seeing their wobbly walk.

Liberty removed her wet gloves and tied them to one of the loops of her cross-body belt. She touched the sore bump on her forehead and studied her fingers. The bleeding had stopped.

She waited while a Loyalist riding a clockwork horse steered through the middle of the roadway. Its joints creaked and the sound of iron horseshoes rang as it progressed. The person used red ribbons to steer the creature.

The physical exhaustion of controlling such a heavy beast was for many easier than riding a flesh horse. Technologists believed that the massive holes left behind with each metal footstep was marginally better than the gastrointestinal feculence of a live horse wreaking havoc on common roads and byways.

Some old-timers still kept flesh horses for winter work as they were not susceptible to rust. Liberty had never had a horse of any kind. She had never had enough money for even a donkey, and her old master hadn't thought much of animals But that didn't matter. All that really mattered was her printing press. The colonists took advantage of her press for many reasons, but her true motive was sharing factual news about the local government. She was proud when Patriots conferred with her and secretly created the Federalist Papers.

That's how Liberty was continually among the first to know the latest news, gossip, and shenanigans. And it's how she knew she must be dedicated to the Patriots' cause. Like Ben Franklin said of a segmented snake: Join or Die. Liberty was sure that united colonies could push back the British, back, back, into that dark sea.

She unlocked each set of bolts with a series of secret button presses that unlatched the gears within. She pushed the heavy door in. From habit, she lit the sconce to the right of the door. Her giant printing press took up much of the building. She had worked so hard to achieve her title of Master Printer, and seeing the massive machine never failed to both thrill and comfort her.

Liberty sat at her small chair next to her equally little table where she kept her writing implements. A range of quill feathers stood like arrows pointed down, waiting for the blood of ink to satiate them. She often embellished notices and pamphlets with small drawings, particularly that disjointed snake.

Removing her favorite quill from its tassel tied onto one of the loops on her belt, she placed it flat across the table. Its copper segments shone in the dim candlelight. Her gift from Paul Revere.

Then she smelled something. Not smoke and not soot. Something warm, spicy, and earthy. She slowly slid her right hand into the cubby on the underside of the table and felt the cold metal of her air blaster. When unlatched, compressed air would escape with a jolt, popping off the black marble ball secured in the tip.

She rose, sniffing. Her father had smoked a pipe, and it brought her a mix of memories, compiled with feelings of anger and abandonment. It had been many years since her father had deposited her at the press as an indentured servant. He had died soon after, when his fishing boat succumbed to the murky depths beyond the bay. Liberty felt no sorrow for the drunken man who had always blamed her for her mother's death during her birth. She took a step closer to the printing press and held her breath as she peered around it.

A figure stepped out from the dark. "Secure your weapon, Liberty. You may yet have cause to use it, but not now."

Liberty knew that voice. She trembled.

Chapter 2

"Mr. Jay, is that you?" Liberty's hands shook in excitement.

"Yes, it is I, with important news to print."

"Of course." Liberty's insides rolled with thrill. "Anything I can do to support the cause. But how did you get in here?"

John Jay took Liberty's now free hand. "I have an uncanny way with locks. I am sorry to intrude like this, but I needed to escape the redcoats after the fiasco this morning."

"Yes, I know."

"How do you know?"

"I was there."

Jay appraised her, her soaked clothes, the blood-encrusted bump on her forehead. He patted her on the back. "You are a true Patriot."

Liberty's chest puffed out with pride. Her face flushed with warmth at the compliment. "I wish to join the ranks of the militia and become a Minuteman."

Jay smiled ruefully and shook his head. "Liberty, you are a powerful force in our fight against British tyranny. Your ink, your words, are the best possible way for you to educate and inform the colonists of the news and not the watered-down version you will find elsewhere."

"But I think I would make a fine Minuteman."

"Alas, as much as you are needed, you are still a woman, and fighting physically is simply not in your capacity." Silence hung in the dimness. "I hope you understand."

"I understand too well." If it wasn't for my womanhood, thought Liberty, I could have married Georgia ages ago, while we were still young and carefree.

Liberty lit the sconces. Tin mirrors reflected the light throughout the windowless room.

She prepared her vast sheets of hemp paper and trimmed down the right size for a pamphlet. Then she and Jay wrote an article for the *Gazette* explaining the deplorable acts of the British soldiers that morning, attacking innocent colonists.

The printing press was her passion. She had worked her way up from an orphaned, indentured servant, to an apprentice, and then, shortly before her mentor died, she had become a Master Printer at the age of nineteen. Hard to believe that had been twenty-five years ago. How much the world had changed since then.

She valued the press for the ability to share fair and honest news. Nailed to an ink-stained wall was the paper she was most proud of printing: *The Sheffield Resolve*, a declaration and petition against British tyranny, and also a manifesto of individual rights of the colonists. She thought of her favorite excerpt: "Mankind in a state of nature is equal, free, and has a right to the undisturbed enjoyment of their lives, liberty, and property."

The steam-powered printing press had a flue leading to the chimney. It took some time to warm up, but when it did, it kept the building toasty in the winter and hot in the summer.

Liberty printed the words she and John Jay used to express the horror of the unjust attack.

John handed Liberty a money pouch. "Thank you for your service, once again."

"It is my sacred honor."

"Would you like to share the fruits of hemp with me before I go?"

"No, thank you."

John Jay filled a sack with the freshly printed papers. "I will be back, with your permission."

"As always."

Liberty sat back at her table and read the proof copy of what she and John Jay had created. As she ruminated, it occurred that she *could* help, *was* helping. Even though she still desperately wanted to join the organized and trained Minutemen, her mission of aiding the emancipation of Massachusetts from British rule would have to be different. The press was her way of fighting.

But that weapon had felt good in her hand.

Retribution took many forms, and Liberty knew hers would come soon. As long as both Georgia and her printing press were safe, that was all she really cared about. She would fight to protect her love and her sacred honor.

Boots crunched on the crusty snow outside her print shop. They sounded steady, sure, and heavy.

She had not locked the door when John Jay had left into the twilight. Had he forgotten an important fact for the article?

She rose. Her steps echoed in a way that made her nervous.

The door handle turned before she could touch it.

"Mr. Jay?"

The door burst open with the last breath of winter wind before spring. A rugged man in red entered, with two other British soldiers flanking him.

"I am Lieutenant Kezziah Burch, and I hereby inform you that if you do not comply with the Stamp Act, you will be forced to stop your operation."

Liberty raised an eyebrow. "You mean the Coercive Acts that demolished Massachusetts' colonial charter and replaced it with an unfair military government?"

Lieutenant Burch growled. "That's the one."

Liberty held her breath as she stared him down. Inside, she was seething, furious at the barrage of sycophants standing in her small shop. Acid jumped from her stomach to her throat. She swallowed the nervous burn.

"We have been here before, and you know what you owe us."

Liberty was afraid that if she spoke, she would cry. So she kept her expression blank, undisturbed. She would not give those greedy monsters the satisfaction of seeing her act distressed.

"Madame," said Burch. "What is wrong with your head? You've got quite a bump."

Liberty disgusted herself with her reply. "That's just me, bumping into all these parts." She waved at the hulking metal beast of a machine. She averted her glance as they laughed at the thought of her walking into one of the protruding cranks. How embarrassing, to demean herself with a lie. Still, she realized that the press would not survive without her compliance.

She stepped solemnly to the wall by her desk. How many hours had the gentle tick-tock of this clock kept rhythm in the shop, even when the printing press roared to life?

She carefully opened the glass covering of the cuckoo clock, removed the face, and pulled out a knob. A multicolored model of a bird shot out on the platform. Holding the bird, attached by a retractable gate, she reached to the small compartment behind it. She retrieved a small brown sack and threw it to the Redcoat, who clumsily caught it. He opened the bag and snorted.

"This is not British tender."

"It's all I've got."

"I suppose it will suffice." Burch eyed the contents again. "Follow, men." As he turned to leave, he froze, his eyebrows clenched together. "What is this?"

Liberty followed his eyes to her treasured copy of the *Sheffield Resolve*.

Lieutenant Burch looked at Liberty over his shoulder. He tore down the *Sheffield Resolve*, crumpled it into a ball, and threw it furiously at Liberty. She dodged. The wad of paper fell behind her to the ink-splotched floor.

"Next time I won't miss." The door slammed behind Burch and the candles wavered.

Liberty relocked the door in all manners. She stepped towards the printing press and leaned into it like a foal leans into her mother.

Liberty decided it was better to be broke than to have a powerless press. She raised a hand to her forehead. Yup, still sore.

Liberty reactivated the cuckoo clock and returned to the massive machine. She checked the flue and ascertained it needed more fuel. She added Virginia coal to the fire. It roared back to life.

She had print orders to fulfill. While she worked, she thought about the arrogant Redcoat who had threatened her. She would not be burned again.

Chapter 3

Liberty snuffed out all the candles but one. That little light barely kept the dark of the windowless building at bay.

She gently lowered her body to the floor, and jaggedly slithered, like Benjamin Franklin's "Join or Die" snake.

She untethered the steel brush from its loop beneath the giant press and scraped away the rubble of the day. Then she blew out the candle.

By muscle memory, she solved the lock on the trapdoor, 08–14–36.

Liberty smiled. August 14, 1736 was Georgia's birthday. They had celebrated her last birthday together, and were also together in every fashion that day. That night, being boyishly rugged came in handy for Liberty, as she jumped and pulled herself up onto a maple tree branch and started climbing to Georgia's window.

But tonight she was tired and half frozen. She lifted the brass handle and pulled the trapdoor up. Then she scooted around and lowered herself to the opening. She grasped onto the old knotted ship rope, and climbed down until she felt hard ground beneath her shoes.

She lit a candle, and its flame reflected on a large shiny tray. Then she added stiff branches and a slender log to the cast iron stove. The flue went up through the ceiling and out the same chimney as the printing press.

The shop's living quarters were dug out beneath the floor. Warm in the winter and cool in the summer, it was cozy, and dark. Liberty had resided in this room since her apprenticeship ended and her master, her mentor, died. No more sleeping in a corner by the press for her!

She removed a flask of water from her belt and took a deep draught. She lifted a tin pan to appraise her face in the firelight.

"That does not look good." Liberty poked the bump on her forehead and winced. She replaced the tray on the hearth. Opening a small pantry, she took out a brown box of hard biscuits. She made coffee on the fire and ate slowly. If this was to be her only meal, she was going to savor it.

Tomorrow she would tend to her wound. Tonight, she was just too tired.

"Maybe Georgia was right. I am getting too old for this."

Chapter 4

Liberty spun Georgia in a gentle arc.

"This is not a ballroom, silly!" Georgia adjusted her bonnet.

The morning sun felt good against Liberty's back as she and Georgia walked through melting snow and mucky trails along the rows of shops. They passed Light-Q, the inventor who fabricated ingenious self-lighting candles using discarded metal and gadgetry. Then Boo's Creations. The shop door was decorated in mosaics made by Boo herself with beads made from shells she had traded with the Native people.

Liberty grinned and helped Georgia back into the Rocker. Invented by Benjamin Franklin, this mode of transportation was typically used by Patriots. British eyebrows rose when Governor Thomas Hutchinson commissioned one for his daughter's use. Even though he was a Loyalist, appointed by the British government, the governor admired Yankee ingenuity.

"This is living." Liberty leaned back in her rocker with her legs stretched out on the footpads. Then she let her knees bend and rocked back again.

"Easy for you to say, all you have to do is soothe yourself like an infant. I'm the one who has to steer! Oh, cruuuuuud!"

Liberty instantly beheld the situation. She sprung from her chair, maintaining balance by crouching in the small space between the chairs.

Georgia grasped the knobs affixed to the arms of her rocking chair, which was in the locked position. "The knobs are stuck!"

Liberty leaned in with her full weight and pushed the right knob forward, swinging the vehicle towards the left, narrowly missing a well-packed horse being led by its owner. She heard the whinny and hoped the dumb beast at least had the built-in desire for self-preservation.

"Phew, that was a close one!" Liberty fell back into her chair and rested her knees. The wooden gears beneath the seats were already getting worn, but they were simple enough to change out. She began rocking slowly.

Georgia stared intently at the roadway, her hands shaking with adrenaline from the near-miss. "I don't know why they still allow live creatures to exist in cities. They just make a mess, and are loud, smelly, and unprogrammable."

"I've never owned a horse, but I always thought it would feel glorious to ride, a breeze in my face, our shadow impressive against the green fields."

Georgia glanced at Liberty. "You have the most lovely way of making the offensive, desirable."

Liberty turned away from her daydream and focused on rocking again. "Lookout for the—"

"I see it." Georgia pushed hard against both knobs. "Slower."

Liberty minded her lover and eased up more on the rocking.

They passed a Spinster 4.2 stuck with a broken paddle in a small stream of melting muddy snow, right in front of Knox's Bookshop. Liberty craned her neck but didn't see any sign of Mr. Knox or his oxen. Must be closed to farm today, she thought.

Another Spinster 4.2 was directly in front of them now. Wide paddles notched together with spinning wheels, a massive spool of hemp yarn spun through rivets, were held together on a triangular frame. Between the wheels was a platform with a bucket rim held up by two spindly arms to turn the wheels on a triangular frame. The driver expertly held onto the hoop for balance as he stepped down upon a block with one leg, as the other leg standing upon another block rose up, and then that leg pressed down, causing the other one to rise. This manipulated the contraption to drive through the mush of wet snow or the sloppy roadway.

Georgia followed slowly behind. Liberty reached over and rubbed the long cloak covering Georgia's thighs. "The rocking chair was such a strange invention in the first place. But *this* makes sense."

Georgia kept her eyes ahead of her but smiled. Liberty maintained her palm's soft pressure on her leg.

"Georgia, you should get your father to buy a rocking chair for your room. I'm starting to get ideas."

Georgia smiled through her blush.

"Well, anyway, this Rocker Roller with the larger seats was really the way to go."

Liberty and Georgia stopped at the far ends of the shops. Georgia looked around nervously.

"What's the matter?" asked Liberty.

"I'm just a bit overwhelmed."

"Is it because you are not accustomed to doing your own shopping?"

"My father is constantly working these days, meeting with dignitaries, creating even more household work to be done for the Governor's mansion. More dignitaries mean more meals, mean more tableware, mean more cleaning, mean more cooking, mean more shopping, mean more work and less time..."

"Wow, that all sounds like a lot! No wonder why you wanted to use the Rocker Roller today."

"Doing my part as lady of the household is important, but stressful. Father and I only see each other in passing, and when I have seen him lately, he seems morbid. Could be that it is the anniversary of my mother's and brother's death from measles. I still can't believe so much time has passed."

"I'm sorry. I know how painful it is to grow up with parts of your family missing." Liberty drifted into her own thoughts. Fiercely independent, she believed that her hardships had led her to the life she was meant to lead. Sometimes Georgia seemed a little out of touch and spoiled, but that was because her father doted on her. Now, however, with tensions between the Loyalists and the Patriots rising, Georgia's duties as the lady of the mansion had increased. Liberty was thrilled to have some time alone with her, even if it was just doing errands together.

They stepped into the general store. The owner motioned Liberty over to the counter. "I've got something you might be interested in."

"I'm curious! Let's see!"

Georgia searched the shelves for items while Liberty approached the counter.

The store-keep rummaged through the shelves beneath the counter. Finally, the keep lifted a long, shiny tube.

"It couldn't be. You have some of Paul Revere's rolled copper?"

"New to market, and I had a feeling you would make good use of it."

"Thank you! This saves me time, and aggravation too." She slipped her fingers under her blue wool hat and lightly brushed her fingers across the lump on her forehead.

The shop-keep nodded. "I only go into Boston because I have to, to collect goods. But I stay far away from that cursed water, and anything red."

Liberty chuckled. "Very wise choices." She paid for her purchase and slung the rolled copper over her right shoulder. She glanced at Georgia. "I'll meet you outside where I am less likely to knock things over."

Outside, Liberty used both arms to wrangle the awkward roll of copper. What a treasure! She began thinking about all the ways she could use it for her press.

She heard her beloved calling out "thank you" as she left the store.

"Did you find everything you needed?" asked Liberty.

"Almost. I was quite aghast to learn there was no tea!"

Liberty appraised her lover's fancy red cloak and soft bonnet perfectly framing her pretty face and the look of consternation in her eyes. She started laughing. "My darling, this side of the glade doesn't use tea."

"Not since the incident with the tea?"

Liberty's face clouded over. "Not since the Motherland demanded outrageous tariffs for it."

"You know I am not as conservative as my father is. But even I don't much care for London."

Liberty maneuvered the rolled copper in between the grand rocking chairs. "Why not?"

"Because they do not care much for us."

Liberty mulled that over. "The French care about us."

"Yes, to eat what bread we make! They just want the colonies to be separated from Great Britain so they can acquire more land for themselves!"

"Wouldn't you say so about the Spanish, too?"

"If they hadn't been so helpful in the South, we might all be eating croissants right now."

"I like croissants," Liberty said.

"That's not the point, my dear."

Liberty stepped back from the Rocker Roller so she could help Georgia onto the vehicle. She glanced back at the general store to see a rivet woman leaning against the side of the building.

Liberty sighed. “There but for the grace of God go I.”

“What do you mean?”

“I’ll be right back. I’ll talk to you in a minute’s time.” Liberty approached the rivet woman.

“Hello there. I was just shopping and wondered if you had rivets for sale.”

The thin, wan woman squinted into the glare of the sun on melting snow. “I do, I do, and at fair cost. Or trade.” She reached deep into the long sack around her neck. “Small, medium, or large?”

Liberty patted her forefinger on her lips as if contemplating a deal. “How about one satchel of each?”

The poor woman’s eyes lit up. Her grey, loose hair waved in the wind brought on by spring weather.

Liberty paid and the woman gave her three small bags of rivets. “Thank you.”

“Thank you. These are sure to come in handy.”

“May the shadow of the deep never touch you.”

“Likewise, for sure.”

Liberty returned to the Rocker Roller and hoisted herself on.

"What was that about?" asked Georgia. "Is that old woman alright?"

"Just one more minute. We need to figure this out." Liberty fiddled with the rolled copper to make it more secure. "I am worried about it falling when we get started down these streets."

"What if we leave it and come back for it?"

"No, wait, hmm... What if... Yes, I think this will work." Her gaze met Georgia's. She smiled. "Ready for a fun challenge?"

"I don't know Liberty... does it involve us pulling the Rocker Roller all the way back to the mansion?"

"You will be relieved to know it is nothing of the sort. Just settle in, good. Now, here's one end of the roll, if you could lay it across your lap, yes, that's right. And if I can finagle a way to pretzel my body into the seat... There we go!"

"I don't know, this might be too cumbersome to wear it across our laps like this while we stomp and steer."

"It will be a good way to warm up certain muscles that you like to use with me, and which I find to be cozy wrapped around my ears."

"Liberty!" Georgia's scolding voice was followed by immediate laughter. "You can be so crass!"

"I'm just saying sweet nothings to you."

Georgia laughed again. "Can we get on our way now? I think I can handle it."

"Oh, I know you can handle it.

"How about this, we can travel to the press, where I will help you with this cumbersome copper. Then I will go solo back to the mansion and unpack all my treasures."

"Good plan."

They rocked and rolled out towards the press. "What was going on with that old woman back there, whom you called a rivet woman?"

Liberty fingered the soft, small bags of rivets. "A rivet woman is a fatherless widow without any kin. I am no widow, though I might as well be one!" She smiled, imagining the curve of Georgia's thighs. "She is a poor woman who sells cheap rivets to passersby to make ends meet. And anyone could make use of a few extra rivets."

"True enough."

"But my dear, there is one shocking piece of information that you don't understand."

"What could that be?" She pulled to the left to avoid a gaggle of live turkeys parading across the road.

"That rivet woman, she is our age!"

"No, that is not possible."

Liberty laughed. “It’s true! Makes me feel a bit better about the silver strands in my hair.”

Georgia kept her eyes on the road but smiled. “You will still be glorious when your red hair turns entirely white.”

Liberty concentrated on her task, but she soaked up the praise.

“Look out!” Liberty reached over to the arm of Georgia’s rocker. She yanked and almost lost her balance as she struggled to keep her behind in her own seat.

A colonist was walking alongside his team, holding the reins in his right hand, keeping his wagon to the right side of the road.

“I swear, Boston drivers are the worst.” Liberty settled in her chair and leaned back slowly. “They don’t even know to cross only at the crosswalk.”

“The horses are beautiful, though.” Georgia squinted at the road ahead of her.

“The Patriots’ mecha-horses have benefits that flesh horses do not possess, though.” Liberty looked at Georgia. “Are you quite right?”

“Yes, just a little shaken up by that close call.”

“You are doing just fine.”

"So, what were you saying about flesh horses?" Georgia glanced at Liberty and smiled to prove she was alright.

"Just that mecha-horses are more equitable. They can be built full size instead of raising or breaking a foal. Can be made as cheaply or gallantly as one's finances allow."

"Or as far as their fashion wills."

"Good point, my dear!"

"I do love horse's beautiful manes though. When I was little, I was always braiding my ponies' hair."

"I bet you were as cute then as you are beautiful now."

"Thank you! Extra kissy points for you today!"

Liberty laughed. "Anything to earn your lovin'! But really, mecha-horses are the way to go. No food or barn fees and cleaning up after them is a cinch. Environmentally friendly as they don't add the mushy mess of horse excrement to the roadways."

Georgia grimaced. She preferred not to talk or think about crude subjects.

A large, curved barricade swung open like a door. Georgia and Liberty came close but managed not to slam into it, instead stopping just inches from the splintered moving wall.

"Here we go, perfect example," said Liberty. "This part of the intersection has been closed off so that errand-doers can cross without becoming a permanent part of the street. Next, when they have passed, we simply tug at the pulley wheel until it opens again. Flesh horses stamp their hooves and whinny and must be coaxed out onto the roadway again. Mecha-horses—all you need to get them going is program their gears ahead of time, and jack the pewter tail up and down to recoil the pulleys and tighten the gears."

"I agree with most of your points. But I maintain that flesh horses are prettier."

Both women laughed. "Well, I have ridden neither in my life and have no opinion on beauty. Only yours."

"Are you saying I am at least as pretty as a flesh horse?"

"At least."

The two women laughed again.

Chapter 5

Liberty and Georgia slowed to a halt in front of the printing press. Liberty glanced at the meager one-level, well-kept, windowless building. She thought of Georgia's home, the Governor's Mansion, where she held the title of Lady of the House. Liberty was no pauper, but she certainly did not live the privileged lifestyle of a governor's daughter.

Liberty rose to hug Georgia and to sneak a kiss on her cheek, shaded by her large bonnet. Then she grappled with the shiny rolled copper and stood back as Georgia waved goodbye.

No sooner had Liberty pulled herself back up from her quarters beneath the hulking press than there was a firm knock at the door. She opened it, and her stomach roiled. "What do you want?"

Lieutenant Burch snarled. "Still miffed after four years of the rightful Stamp Act?"

Liberty said nothing and pulled her heavy ink-stained leather apron over her head.

Burch said to one of his men, “That’s what they are like. Too thick to understand what is going on.”

“I know what’s going on. A tyrant is using his power to claim people as his own. Well, not me. I’m free.”

Burch stepped toward her. His foul breath washed over Liberty. “If you want to keep your freedom, you’d better start cooperating.”

Liberty stared him down. “There is no man to whom I would surrender my freedom.”

“I’d be careful if I were you.”

“What is it? What are you asking me for this time?”

Burch pushed a scroll into her hand. Liberty pulled her multi-goggles, Ben Franklin’s finest, from one of her pockets across the chest of the apron. She slid the goggles onto her face and adjusted the magnifiers over each lens by turning screws to make the ocular lenses rotate. Then she pulled a lever from the bridge of the goggles, lifting small bent metal arms affixed with tiny mirrors. With these, she could read and lay the smallest print.

“You’d like me to print your tax notice?” Liberty grimaced.

“More like, *you* will do your duty and print it, in honor of the Crown.”

"You mean you want me to print your tax notice *for free*?"

Lieutenant Burch leaned on the giant printing press. Liberty sucked in her breath. What if Burch saw the article she was typesetting for John Jay! She hoped Burch would not be able to read the backwards typeset and see the newest Federalist Papers. She eyed the ink staining the side of Burch's red coat with each shift of his body and said nothing. Sometimes things were funnier when kept to oneself.

"I mean, if you like your hovel to remain intact, don't bite the hand that feeds you."

"The hand that feeds me? I survive because I refuse to pay your high tariffs, and I boycott British goods. I eat because of my community, my home, my country."

Burch pushed the scroll into Liberty's hands. "You'd be wise to shut your trap of a mouth before you snag a beast you can't out-talk." He stomped off towards the still-open door, his two men trailing him. "I will be back this afternoon."

Liberty sat at her small table and assessed her choices

She regarded the message the soldier wanted printed—for free. Memories of previous discrepancies amused her: the time she printed a snarky headline on the Redcoats' banner, or when she made an "unfortunate mistake." What shall she do this time...

When Lieutenant Burch returned, Liberty had left the heavy door open and was leaning over the press with her big leather apron on, focused on her next job. There were constant news updates that the Patriots needed printed. She was glad to do her part and make a dependable income.

Without looking up, Liberty said, "I have not completed the work."

Burch's tone was brusque. "Show me what you have thus accomplished."

Liberty reached into the large tool bag at her hip. Her fist came out tightly clenched. In a quick jerk, she swung her arm like a young girl feeding chickens, moving her arm as if she were scattering seeds.

Burch jumped, immediately furious with embarrassment. "What are you doing, crazy lady?"

"I'm giving you all that you'll get from me. Scat! Shoo!"

"Print this or pay the consequences!"

Liberty continued typesetting rows of letters for the next job. Spelling helped her remember everything that she printed.

Burch was infuriated at being ignored. "Are you inept, or simply mad?"

"Just a woman doing her job."

Lieutenant Burch spat on the floor. Liberty's stomach churned. Men were so gross. "Print it; my men need it."

Liberty kept on her typesetting. "I didn't know so many of you were literate."

In a flash of red, Burch was at her back and grabbing her braid. "You don't want to lose your head, do you?"

Liberty shook in fear and indignity. She was too shocked to speak.

He released his grip and spun away. "One hour, woman. Or else."

Liberty kept her back to the door and waited until she heard it close. She braced herself against her beloved machine, tucked her chin to her chest, and stiffly lowered herself to the floor. She knelt huddled under her big apron, covered her face, and cried heaving, silent tears.

Finally, she stood and dried her face with an ink-stained cloth she kept notched to her apron's belt. Then she took a deep breath and resigned herself to completing the task, still shaking. Errant tears trickled down her face. Liberty was angry, mostly at herself. She wanted to defend her beliefs, but needed to protect the press. If the only way to get the Redcoats out of her hair was to succumb, then she would. She could see no other choice. But someday, she promised herself, she would stand up to all of them.

Chapter 6

Liberty stood naked before Georgia's full-length mirror. She saw Georgia's reflection from the bed.

"Nice view," said Georgia.

Liberty met her eyes in the mirror and grinned.

"Would you like to lounge some more?" asked Georgia.

"Lounge? Is that what we are calling it now?"

Georgia giggled.

Liberty twisted to see her backside in the mirror.

"Look all you like," said Georgia. "I know I am surely enjoying what I see."

"I have a scheme and need an outfit to make it work."

Georgia began redressing, one ladylike layer at a time. "How can I help?"

"Well, I, umm... need a skirt."

"A skirt? You?"

Liberty shifted her eyes to the rug. All four corners of the room had bolts affixed to the floor. Hemp rope looped around them and pulled the rug taut to keep it from moving and bunching up. "Yes."

Georgia's blue eyes brightened with curiosity. "I could certainly hire a seamstress. Or better yet, I could create something special for you myself."

"I do not want anything fancy. In fact, I need the opposite of fancy."

Georgia smoothed down her bed linens. "What do you need a skirt for?"

"I am not sure it is prudent to share right now."

"A mystery? Or are you keeping a handsome man on the side? Perhaps that hunk of a Frenchman, the Marquis de Lafayette?"

Liberty turned to her and raised her eyebrows. "You are so strange sometimes."

"I'm strange? You're the one asking for a skirt! Which shouldn't be odd, but for you, Liberty, a skirt?"

"It need not be a new one. In fact, the older the better."

Georgia frowned in disappointment. "If you are going to wear a skirt, you deserve a new one."

"No, really, for my purposes, I would prefer something more subtle, less elaborate, plain."

Georgia's eyes narrowed. "Does this have something to do with stirring up rebel trouble?"

Liberty closed her eyes and blew out her breath between her lips.

Georgia's voice went flat. "Fine, don't tell me."

Liberty gritted her teeth, anxiously searching her brain for a viable excuse. But she would not lie to her beloved. She sighed. "I suppose I do owe you the truth."

"Wait, no. Maybe I am better off not knowing."

Liberty's forehead wrinkled. She met her lover's eyes hopefully. "So, you will help me?"

Georgia paused. "How could I not?"

Liberty embraced her. "Thank you."

"Careful now, temptress, you're going to get me all riled up again. Not that I mind your bare skin beneath my hands."

Liberty grinned, then turned back to the mirror, trying to imagine herself in womanly clothes. She could barely remember the last time she had worn a skirt. Probably that fateful day when her father abandoned her.

Georgia sat on the edge of the bed, her eyes on Liberty's reflection. "I must admit, I am scared because I see guilt in your eyes, and I also see determination. If I can't be privy to your secret, then I suppose I can at least make the burden of it easier for you." She rose to her wardrobe and opened the wide door. "Since you persist on evading a new garment, perhaps you would like to pick something from my collection?"

Liberty peeked into the wardrobe. All colors of the rainbow were represented in Georgia's fine skirts.

Georgia rifled through the clothes and pulled out a skirt with a pattern in the shade of clear skies. "I think blue is your color."

"That is very pretty, but I am looking for something less pretty. Do you have anything in brown?"

"I have a brown apron. Would that work?"

"Yes, that would be perfect. But I still need a skirt. And perhaps a shirt."

Georgia grabbed Liberty's hand. "I would be delighted to sew something for you! We can use some of the finest fabrics that Father has imported!"

"Me, using imported fabric."

"Yes, from the homeland."

"You mean the oppressors."

"I mean," said Georgia lightly, "that I am a British subject. Father did state an oath to the Crown after all."

"Yes, when he was made *Governor*." Liberty rolled her eyes.

"Darling, I thought we agreed to disagree on certain matters of politics."

"But this is not political, it is life!"

"Yes, and right now I would like to create a skirt for you."

"Not fancy. It must be plainer than your servants' clothing."

"Here we go then," said Georgia, gently smiling at Liberty. "This skirt has not fit me in years, since my body has become more ample."

"And beautifully so."

"If I take it in at the waist and shorten the hem, I think it will suit you just fine."

Liberty sat on the end of the bed next to Georgia. "I still need time to recover from our fun." She squeezed Georgia's hand and lay back on the bed.

"And I must measure and mark!" She stepped past her bookshelf. She unlatched a drawer of her tall bureau and removed measuring tape and a journal to jot down Liberty's physical statistics.

A few hours later, after a small luncheon for two was delivered by a knowing servant to the bedroom, Georgia declared she was finished.

Liberty tried on a plain blue skirt, adjusted for her compact frame, pulled over the white shirt Georgia had offered, and tied the brown apron.

Georgia's face glowed. "You are beautiful, even in dowdy clothes, but forgive me," she covered her smile with one hand. "You, you," she gasped for breath between bursts of laughter, "standing there in a skirt with no bloomers on! Easy access!"

Liberty's scowl in the mirror turned into a smile. "You are never satiated, are you."

"You always keep me wanting more! But truly, it is a wonder to see you dressed so feminine. Oh wait, one more thing!" She undid Liberty's masculine braid, tied back in a blue bow. She carefully rearranged her style to be more feminine. "Your hair is so beautiful."

"Thank you." Liberty's eyes were closed as she luxuriated in the feeling of Georgia's soft brush against her scalp.

"Now look," said Georgia.

Liberty twirled in front of the tall looking glass. She almost didn't recognize herself.

Liberty turned and gave her beloved a massive hug. "This is just right, thank you."

"My absolute pleasure."

Liberty turned to the window to leave. She hiked up her skirt and felt the chilly mid-spring air swirl upwards.

"Liberty, are you sure you can climb in your current attire?"

Wind whipped Liberty's skirt straight up. "I can easily put my own clothes back on."

"You could, or you could finally walk down the stairs and out the front door like a proper woman."

"Like a proper woman!" Liberty laughed. Then she saw Georgia's patient smile. "You're not kidding?"

"Maybe I'm half kidding."

Liberty nodded.

"Just think, you are dressed appropriately, well, for an old beggar woman."

"I'm not old!"

"You're no beggar woman either."

"Thanks for that!" The two women shared a laugh. Liberty stepped away from the window. She changed out of the new attire and quickly put her own clothes on.

"How are you going to bring your new garments with you?"

Liberty took the garments that Georgia had picked up from the floor. She glanced at the tree outside the window. Then she stuffed the folded skirt, shirt, and apron down her white button-up shirt.

Georgia laughed.

"What's so funny?"

"You look almost as fat as that lout Benjamin Franklin! Now all you need is a harem of French girls!"

Liberty grinned. "There's only one gal for me, and she is a glorious woman who can outwit any French lady." She headed to the window again.

"I truly hope you are doing the right thing, whatever it is. Just don't run off with Lafayette!"

Liberty smiled at Georgia's teasing tone. "I'm not leaving you."

Georgia smiled back. "I know there's no one else. Besides the rebels."

Liberty winced. She wished Georgia could understand how important it was to her to aid the Patriots in their shared value set.

"Please promise me you will be safe."

"I will be." Liberty pushed the window further up on its rope runners.

Georgia followed Liberty to the window. "The new outfit really will all look lovely on you."

Liberty straddled the windowsill. "One last kiss for luck?"

Georgia cupped Liberty's cheeks in her hands and kissed her long and deep.

Liberty exhaled heavily. "That's a lot of luck!" She shimmied down the tree, allowing gravity to help her. Then she sprinted beyond the mansion's gardens and took off for her home.

Chapter 7

Liberty surveyed the British soldiers marching in rhythm to the even tempo of a metronome. It was loud with a big copper funnel at the top and a smooth dowel ticking the beat.

She could feel eyes on her. Or was she simply being paranoid? She took a step closer through the foliage and paused, her eyes roaming the outskirts.

Finally, with a deep breath, Liberty stepped out of hiding. She slowly walked the circumference of the camp. Her skirt swished with each step. The soldiers ignored her. She wondered if perhaps she was dressed too well for her ruse.

She was just thinking about slinking back out of the enemy camp when a voice called out. "Woman, you look like you could warm up. Why don't you join us at the fire?"

Liberty assessed the situation. Four long logs were set up in a square, with a small cozy fire in the middle. Without her coat, this early spring day chilled her.

"Don't turn your back on a fire." The soldier smiled warmly and motioned for Liberty to join him and two others who were leaning forward in conversation. "I'm Sergeant Joseph Woods."

Liberty's heart pounded. This was the chance she was waiting for. She took a few steps closer.

"Come now, do not be afraid. What kind of gentlemen would we be if we didn't offer our warmth to a woman?"

"We've got plenty of warmth," chuckled one soldier, with a twinge of danger in his voice.

Liberty sat on the end of the log that formed a corner with Sergeant Woods's seat.

She smiled politely, then her smile froze. She recognized Sergeant Woods as the one leading the British in the mob attack in which she had been injured. Her forehead still bore the fading yellow and purple bruise.

"Men, we have a lady visitor here. And I suppose she has some purpose rather than our mere entertainment." He looked pointedly into Liberty's eyes. "So?"

Liberty reached into the long satchel at her neck. She pulled out a small pouch of rivets. "I offer a variety of high-quality rivets for sale." She passed the rivets to Woods.

He clasped them in his hand and considered his options. Liberty needed to gain control of the situation before he decided he didn't want a rivet woman in the camp.

"I will gladly trade them for some food and drink."

"Sold!" Sergeant Woods pocketed the rivets and motioned for food and red wine to be brought over.

Liberty ate in silence while Woods turned back to the other men in conversation. She chewed her bread slowly. Although she seemed focused on her meager meal, really she was listening to the redcoats speaking amongst themselves.

She knew that if she could continue this ruse, and kept her ears open and mouth closed, she would be able to collect useful information to bring to the Minutemen. Then they would let her join them!

Day after day she returned to the camp, where she had come to be a regular face among the crowd.

Sergeant Woods greeted her on the seventh day. "Look who it is! Madame Rivets!" The other soldiers chuckled.

There was a larger group on the log encampment, eating and chatting. Woods sat next to Liberty.

"I have something of great value to share with you all today." His voice projected over the small fire. The other men paused to see what he was talking about.

Liberty was curious too. Maybe it was news she could take back to the Minutemen!

Woods reached into his satchel and pulled out a red silk cloth wrapped around an unidentifiable object. He held it in one hand and neatly pulled the scarf away. “Behold, the soundbox!”

The other soldiers laughed.

Liberty was confused. “Pardon me, but what is a soundbox?”

Sergeant Woods leaned over so she could see it better. “See that bumpy cylinder in the middle of the box? And the metal prongs?”

Liberty nodded.

“When the soundbox is wound up, like so,” he rotated the handle on the outside of the box, “the cylinder slowly turns. As it does, the bumps hit the metal prongs, creating pleasing musical sounds.” He stopped winding, slid a switch, and the cylinder started incrementally spinning.

“What is its purpose?”

“Why, to sing and dance to, of course!”

One of the redcoats across the fire grumbled. “I’m too worn out from drills to dance. And believe me, you do not want to hear me sing.” The other soldiers laughed good-naturedly.

“Wait, I’ve got just the song!” Woods reached into a pocket in his side satchel. He pulled out another cylinder like the one currently playing a tinny tune. He examined it, tracing his fingers along the bumps. His face lit up with mischief. "This is the one!"

He switched out one cylinder for another, wound the soundbox, and shifted the switch. A bright and happy tune began to play.

"I like this jaunty melody, but I do not recognize it." Liberty cocked her head.

The soldiers around the fire laughed. One almost choked on his food.

Woods smirked. "C'mon, someone, sing along!"

Mead was passed and a young soldier stood. "I shall siiing!"

The group clapped and chortled encouragingly.

Yankee Doodle went to town

riding on a pony

Stuck a feather in his cap

And called it macaroni!

The entire group started laughing.

Liberty smiled even though she was confused. She had to play the part of a dumb woman, but she also had to know. "That song makes no sense to me. Why would there be French in a British song?"

Sergeant Woods clapped his hands. "That's what makes it especially funny!"

"Play it again, please."

"Yes, Madame Rivets."

This time, when Liberty recognized the chorus of the song, she stood and sang. The redcoats went wild with laughter.

She sat back down, a little out of breath. Her hands were shaking, though she felt brave, not scared.

"Dear woman, I do believe this soundbox was meant for you, in honor of your quiet company and surprising entertainment value. And for having perfect attendance of late, unlike many of these soldiers here."

The other men guffawed and went back to their conversations.

"Thank you." Liberty took leave of the encampment and meandered her way home. She was sure she had accumulated enough information to report to the Minutemen. She had the redcoats' trust now. She didn't know how far that trust would take her, but she had a feeling her life was about to take a drastic change.

Chapter 8

Georgia was delighted to see Liberty at her window.

They held each other and kissed. They were quiet for several moments, simply enjoying the joy of each other's touch.

"I cannot stay long."

Georgia was crestfallen. "You cannot spend the afternoon? I'll have a servant serve luncheon."

"Not today, but soon, I promise."

"Dare I ask where you are going today?"

"I cannot lie to you or deny you important information about my life. Someday I will tell you all about it. But this," she reached into the bag attached to the belt around her waist and fluffed the skirt within, "must remain a secret. For now."

Chapter 9

Liberty approached the Minuteman training camp. She felt much more comfortable in her more masculine clothes and felt the spring sun on her face as she walked to the edge of the countryside.

She glanced around the camp, looking for an officer of high rank, known by a cockade decorating his tricorn hat.

Finally, she saw a man with a spinning gear in the middle of a red, white, and blue ribbon on his tricorn hat. He must be in charge.

She gathered up her courage, took a deep breath, and confidently sauntered over. "Sorry to interrupt, as I know you are busy training the Minutemen for battle, as necessary and needed."

The leader appraised her. "I kindly accept your pluck, but I don't think you were created to be a soldier."

"But I would be a terrific Minuteman."

"Key word, *man.*"

"You can call me Bert. I am more manly than the young boys you are training."

"Bert... it takes more than desire to be a Minuteman." He went back to his pipe.

"With all respect, Minutemen are known for their ability to assemble quickly. I am quick and agile. And the Minutemen's main advantage lies in familiarity with the land. Which I definitely have."

The man softened. "We could always use spinners to provide the raw material to make cloth for our uniforms."

Liberty studied admiringly his bright yellow and green striped uniform and wistfully eyed the tricorn hat. Then she looked up at the leader again. Their eyes met. She could see the crinkle lines circling his soft brown eyes as he winked.

"Thank you for stopping by."

"Wait, please, one more minute, I have important news for you!"

The man sighed in exasperation. Yet he was clearly intrigued. "What is it?"

"The British are sending a fleet of waterships offshore to ensure safety for the Loyalists, so the Patriots do not try their tea dumping again. And the ships are full of Redcoats so they can patrol more safely past the streets of Boston, to the countryside, where they will no longer be outnumbered."

"How did you gain this information?" The leader clearly was suspicious of this woman dressed as a man.

"I have secretly been gleaning information from the enemies. Sometimes being a woman comes in handy. But that's not all the news I have about the British waterships. Once they unload their military cargo, they plan on keeping the ships in the bay, essentially cutting off the Boston Harbor from any other trade."

The leader's eyes squinted in thought. "But the French..."

"I know the French are our greatest allies, along with the Spanish. And of course the Wampanoag, who have always been allies."

"Allies is a strong word in wartime."

Liberty nodded. She stood with both feet firmly planted on the ground, implying a sense of confidence. But inside she was shaking. What if she was not accepted after all her hard work? At least she would have gotten her message through, and that was most important, she reasoned.

The leader took another puff of his pipe then turned to the side to blow out the ash. He looked into Liberty's face again. "I appreciate your distinctive ability to secure this information and report it to me. It will surely be helpful to us and our cause. I cannot hire you as a Minuteman. However, let me encourage you to report back to me with further discoveries about the British plans."

Liberty agreed. Then, with dignity, she left the site of the training men. She felt deflated, but relieved that her information would be useful to the Patriots.

Chapter 10

Liberty put her feet in the stirrups of the tricycle. “Are you sure about this?”

Georgia adjusted her goggles from the side box on wheels, attached to the trike with a pewter bar. “Father doesn’t pay any mind to which modes of transportation I use, and we have so many. He is so busy with trying to govern in this incredible political turmoil. And I could use a break.”

Liberty turned knobs on the large dashboard in front of her. The gears interacted, and the wheels started moving, pulling the side box heavily along.

“My view is the exhaust of horses.” Georgia covered her mouth with her white apron.

“That’s my view of the Redcoats!”

Georgia laughed good-naturedly.

Liberty adjusted the speed by spinning a knob on the control panel. "I hear the Hessians are causing conflict with the Redcoats."

"You would know, investigator of all things political!" Georgia kept her apron to her face.

"Well, the Redcoats can have their allies, but the Patriots have allies too."

"I wish you could imagine, for just a moment, that the British are vying for peace with law and order. Not a war."

Liberty cruised bumpily along. "The Redcoats are not the allies of the colonies. They are oppressors. The Patriots are outnumbered. Even the local Native tribes are split between sides. This totalitarian government rule we are under involves the whole world. Our rights hang in the balance." Liberty shifted gears. "We are on the edge of a revolution. Do you understand?"

"I do understand. That is why I am terrified."

"Of the Crown losing power?"

"That, and the chaos that war carries." Georgia paused. "But mostly I am afraid of being separated from you. I am incredibly anxious when you are not with me, when you are gone, and there is no accounting for the hours you spend away."

"I love you, even when we aren't on the same side."

"I know that. Yet the impact of your choice to keep something from me is devastating."

Liberty winced with guilt at her lover's words. They bounced on slowly.

Georgia broke the silence. "You truly believe that thirteen colonies could disrupt such a powerful empire?"

"Yes."

"How?"

"The Redcoats may have us outnumbered, and out-weaponed. But that only shows how afraid they are. And they should be. The Patriots aren't fighting for the cause of money or power. We are fighting for dignity, freedom, and our homes!"

"You truly believe yourself to be one of them?"

"Were I a man, I would be accepted into their barracks. Even if I were a mere boy, I would be awarded the honorable opportunity to join the rebel forces. Well, I'll tell you something. I refuse to be doomed to a life of spinning a wheel of thread, just because of what I bear beneath my knickers."

This last bit made Georgia giggle. "You are awfully crass sometimes. It is rather unexpected. But I suppose I should know to expect no less from you."

"I meant no offense."

"None taken, my dearest."

They traveled on in thoughtful peace. Liberty maneuvered the contraption with slow and steady attention. In due time, she reached the end of the lane before the broad road that led to the governor's mansion.

Liberty unstrapped herself and lowered herself from the trike. Then she gallantly unhooked the door to the side box and leaned forward to assist Georgia.

Georgia's eyes shifted to the barn. Nobody was about. Liberty read Georgia's expression. She leaned in and kissed her mouth.

"Heck with it!" exclaimed Georgia. "Go climb the tree to my bedroom!"

"In the height of noon?"

"Nobody will see."

Liberty grinned. "It is you who is naughty after all."

Liberty kept still and watched Georgia ride the trike the rest of the way to the barn. Liberty slunk to the large oak tree. She pulled herself up to her lover's bedroom, their sanctuary.

Chapter 11

The warmth of her lover's body left her upon seeing Lieutenant Burch pacing angrily in front of the print shop when Liberty arrived home that afternoon. The officer pushed a scroll into Liberty's hands.

Liberty glanced at the latest declaration from the Crown. "What makes you think I would print this for you?"

Burch's breath came hot and fast in her face. "Because it is your duty to serve the Crown." Liberty winced but didn't back away. "I shall return before the end of day."

Liberty was crestfallen. She had other plans this evening, namely to tuck into a good stew and resign herself to desperately needed sleep. Her whole body ached from her first-ever trike ride.

She added more fuel to the fire. It served the press to be kept warm and ready. And it heated the large room.

She sat at her desk for just a moment to catch her breath. And quickly dozed off.

She was awakened by pounding on her door. It was dark in the shop, except for the light from the fire. She stretched her hands across her desk almost blindly, found a candle, and lit it. The pounding on the door continued unceasingly. Liberty began to sweat. She knew there was a Redcoat on the other side, and she had not even begun the task he had thrust upon her.

She opened the door, and a rush of red streamed in. Lieutenant Burch had brought three comrades this time. Liberty's breath caught in her throat. She could sense danger in them. They were not making a courtesy call.

"Where is the document?" Burch demanded.

Liberty kept her cool. "It is not complete."

Burch stepped close to her. She could smell body odor emanating from his wool coat. "Do you have any idea of what sort of trouble you are facing?"

Liberty looked up at him and planted her hands on her hips. "I know what's going on. A tyrant is using his power to claim people as his own. Well, not me. I am free."

Burch sneered. "Lucky you are the right skin color to say that. At least in the colonies' idea of freedom."

Liberty's face burned with the truth of his words.

"If you want to keep this freedom of yours, you had best begin cooperating."

Liberty stared up at him. "I will not cooperate with tyranny."

"I'd be cautious if I were you. Right, men?"

The three other Redcoats crowded around Liberty and glowered at her, arms crossed.

"I have given you multiple chances to comply. Each time, you are more and more difficult. I consider this last discrepancy of yours to be an act of treason."

Liberty's face paled.

"However," continued Lieutenant Burch in false friendliness, "since you are of the weaker sex, I have no plans to hang you. You will however, suffer the consequences." He glanced around the circle of sycophants. "Men, you know what to do."

They reached up over their shoulders and pulled heavy objects from their leather knapsacks. Sledgehammers.

Liberty's eyes widened. "No, please no."

"You had plenty of opportunities to conform to proper and lawful standards. Now you must reap what you sow."

Liberty slid to her knees. "Please, anything but that."

Lieutenant Burch ignored her. "Men, do your worst!"

With wicked grins highlighted monstrously in the glow of the printing press, the Redcoats lifted their sledgehammers on their shoulders and swung mightily.

Liberty watched as her press was broken, piece by piece. Hot tears streamed down her face as her body shook with anger. She rose to her feet and lunged for the ink tray, heaving it towards the exuberant destroyers. A thick black arc flew through the clamor and covered Burch from face to feet with ink.

"You she-dog!" he screamed, wiping his eyes with his red sleeves.

The room became brighter as the press's fire grew stronger. Orange flames glinted in the leader's eyes. "Fire. That's it, men! Good work! Now let's burn this building of ill repute down to the ground!"

"Hurrah!" shouted the soldiers. "For the Crown!"

One of the men pried open the metal fireplace cover with the handle of his sledgehammer. Then he reached for the coal shovel that Liberty kept conveniently close by. Another Redcoat pulled scrolls from a box in the corner—Liberty's current workload.

"Over here!" Burch called, motioning towards the blank wall at the back.

The four Redcoats used the scrolls as torches to burn the corners of the walls. Fire ravaged the building.

"Get out, men, before it collapses!" The Redcoats left, with Burch looking back at Liberty before shutting the door on her.

There was no escape but to follow the Redcoats. Liberty grabbed her quills and stuffed them down the front of her shirt. The metal bits were hot and sharp against her skin. Black smoke filled her lungs. She opened the door and stepped out. She heard a splintering crack and ran down the hill. There, it seemed that half the countryside had gathered to watch the burning spectacle. She stopped and turned to see the walls crashing upon themselves, covering her most precious possession with wild flames.

The Redcoats slithered away, leaving the crowd standing awestruck by the destruction. As the walls became soot, the crowd attempted to placate Liberty with sentiments of sorrow and hope. Yet she stood still, staring, as her life in a flash of fire burned before her eyes.

When the building was a hulk of embers and soot and imploded ink jars, the colonists took their leave. Boo from Boo's Creations offered her home for the night, but Liberty stoically shook her head.

After the crowd cleared, Liberty sat on the dry ground. She was sweating and coughing. Before her was everything she had worked for her entire life. Gone.

Throughout the night, Liberty watched the last embers crackle. She nodded off a few times, slumped over in exhaustion. Smoke blocked the stars, but the waxing moon shone just enough light for her to walk back up the short hill.

Her heart dropped. Her body felt numb. But her thoughts were strongly lucid. She walked slowly along the edges of the smoky mess, assessing the printing press that had fallen into her hidden chamber.

In the debris was the remains of her desk. Her heart raced. Was it still there? She kicked through the hot rubble and saw something gleaming in the dirt. There it was, her white and copper weapon. She lifted the metal blaster and pocketed it, burning her hand in the process.

She found a large well of ink in thick glass that had not exploded. "Now, if only I had some paper."

On the other side of the burning rubble was a flicker of white, like a flag of surrender.

Liberty cautiously stepped around flares of fire that shot up unexpectedly as the flames found more fuel to feed them. She approached the white cloth that flapped in the breeze with a solemn echo. She leaned over and pulled out a long, ratty, torn scrap of sail, a remnant from her father. She had planned to someday sew a new knapsack with it. But she had better use for it now.

She pulled the cloth to the bottom of the hill where the smell of burnt things wasn't as strong. She coughed again, her chest dry and prickly.

Pulling the quills out from her shirt, she laid them on the dirt in front of her. Then she removed a small jar of ink from her pants pocket. Her copper quill caught the light of the moon. Liberty picked it up and set to work.

The next morning, the colonists gawked at the message printed with quill and ink on the torn piece of sail hanging from the surviving chimney in the ruins. .

"Press attacked but not destroyed."

Chapter 12

Liberty raced in the rising sun to the governor's mansion. She needed to confess to Georgia and ask for the shelter she knew Georgia would provide. Even if she could seek refuge in the eaves of the barn, she would be grateful.

She heard the snap of a snare drum and the stomp of feet. Just past the tree line, British soldiers marched with their Union Jack flying high before them. She crept to the back garden, but the red swarm encircled the mansion. The marching approached, footstep by footstep. She leaped into the tree and pulled herself up, swinging her legs over branches, and reached the final bough. She scratched on Georgia's window.

"Liberty, in, quickly." Georgia pulled Liberty in with such frantic force that she tripped and fell across the carpet.

The two women hugged, squeezing each other, their hearts beating in turmoil together.

Liberty crouched and snuck a peek out the window. "There are twelve Redcoats around the circumference of the back gardens. More have surrounded the front of the mansion."

A great pounding banged on the mansion's front door. Unable to decode the locking system, the Redcoats used axes with spinning mechanical blades to cut past the door frame. With a thunderous crash, the door fell into the house, and the swarm shouted *hurrah!*

"They've breeched the mansion!"

"I am afraid you will be trapped now, like me!"

"We will figure a way out of this. Do you know why these regulars are infiltrating the governor's mansion?"

"They told Father they needed larger headquarters, and when Father refused to let them in, they pushed him to the side and came charging in anyway. Then Father locked the door from the inside so more could not enter. Father turned and looked up to see me on the banister and darted his eyes towards my quarters. I got the message—hide!"

The bedroom door burst open. Georgia screamed. Liberty jumped in front of her. She didn't know what fight lay ahead, but she was ready for it.

Chapter 13

Liberty patted down her leather apron's pockets. Gloves, wipe rag, copper quill, blaster. She hunched forward and lifted her elbows. Her whole body was a tight spring. One step, and she would be all over him.

Georgia leapt up and knocked into Liberty.

"Stay back!" screamed Liberty.

But Georgia passed her with open arms. "Father!"

The man locked the door.

Liberty slowly lowered her hands. Everything was moving much too fast. She studied the man who had just entered the room. Brown overcoat, brown vest with embroidered white and orange flowers, open to reveal flouncy ruffles of his high-throated shirt. His grey hair was pulled back with a deep blue bow. He turned and looked from Georgia to Liberty.

"Liberty, this is my father, Governor Thomas Hutchinson."

Liberty didn't know what to do. She offered a hand in a sign of peace. The governor took it.

"It is, of course, good to meet you, finally. I believe I've seen glimmers of copper-colored hair flashing amongst the trees on the property."

The sound of stomping boots echoed up the stairs.

Liberty surveyed the scene frantically. Georgia pushed her desk in front of the door. Hutchinson was fiddling with the curtains behind Georgia's bed.

"To the window," directed Liberty. "I can guide you down one at a time, and then we can run to the countryside where it is safer." She motioned desperately. "Please hurry!"

"But what of the soldiers already in the back?" asked Georgia. "How will we get past them?"

"You two, come here." Hutchinson shook the red velvet cloth.

Georgia rushed to her father's side, but Liberty was more skeptical. "We are not going to be able to hide behind a curtain." The world seemed to swirl around her. Was there no way out?

Georgia pulled her into a gaze. Liberty stepped forward and reached out a hand to hold Georgia's. No matter what happened next, Liberty felt some solace that they would be together. Georgia squeezed her hand.

"That's right, ladies. Watch your step."

"Watch our step?" Liberty was already crowding Georgia and Hutchinson. "There is nowhere else to go."

The door rattled in its frame. The clang of axes reverberated throughout the room.

"Forgive me." Hutchinson pulled Georgia out of Liberty's grasp. He pushed his daughter behind the curtain.

In a second, Liberty was toe-to-toe with him. She looked past him behind the curtain, but Georgia wasn't there. "What have you done with her?"

"You'll soon see." In a massive thrust, he pushed Liberty, and she felt soft velvet brush her cheeks as she fell into darkness.

Chapter 14

Liberty landed with a thud. A tiny light approached her.

"Liberty?"

"Georgia!"

Liberty rose from a heap of old saddle blankets. Georgia handed her a candle and lit another one from a large pile. Footsteps and furniture rumbled from above.

"Where are we?" whispered Liberty. Her breath barely moved the candle.

"I'm not sure, but there seems to be light coming from over there."

Liberty looked where she was pointing.

"Let's follow the light; that's the surest way to get out of the dark."

The two women walked, bent over in the low, tight space. They heard a thud and an exclamation of anger behind them.

"Oh no, they've found us!"

"Head towards the light. I won't let anything happen to you."

Another thud, and a shout of surprise. Liberty could hear men's voices. She couldn't lose Georgia. She would save her, no matter what the cost.

"Look," whispered Georgia. "There's a cellar window! Now we need to find a way up there to get out."

"I'll just lift you, and you move your feet like you are walking up the wall." Liberty struggled to grab Georgia the most effective way.

"Wait, how about these old butter churns? We can stack them up and climb out."

"Brilliantly figured out, dearest!" Liberty's spirit rose again. Now there was a plan. They would escape.

They created a pyramid of wooden conical containers, remnants of a pre-mechanical time.

Liberty held out a hand to Georgia. "Let's get you out of here."

"I would feel safer if you went first. You are the expert climber, after all. I will pay close attention and step and balance just as you do."

Liberty looked up toward the window. “It’s not that high. You’ll do great. Just hurry!” She leaned forward and briefly their lips touched. Then Liberty began her ascent.

She got to the top, jiggled the cobwebbed window open, and peeked out. She didn’t see any Redcoats from her vantage point. It was risky to climb out the window, but even riskier to stay. She turned and knelt towards the window and reached down with two arms. “Almost there,” she encouraged.

Georgia wobbled on the butter churns but kept her balance. Her fingers touched Liberty’s. She smiled in relief.

“I’ve got you!” prodded Liberty.

“No, I’ve got you!” A man with a face as red as his coat grabbed Georgia around the waist and pulled her. She fell to the floor.

“Georgia!”

“Go on without me!”

The brutish man looked towards the window where Liberty was screaming for Georgia to get up. His lips curled back, revealing rotted black gums. He was hunched over in the cramped space, and jumped to try to pull Liberty back in by the arms. She pushed backward just in time.

A second man approached and lifted Georgia from the ground. “Let’s go, I’ve got her.”

“What about the other one?”

"This is Hutchinson's daughter, lady of the house. She is the one we need to get him to comply with us using the mansion as our new base of operations. Let the rabble roll away."

"Liberty! Run!"

The soldier with black gums looked back up toward the window. Liberty was nowhere in sight.

The tamp of their feet as they pulled Georgia along left footprints among the mouse prints. Liberty held her breath where she was frozen back against the brick of the mansion. Her heart pounded and her eyes poured silent hot tears. She had failed. She had lost Georgia. But she would get her back! She peered back into the window. No one was there. Maybe she could sneak back in, retrieve Georgia, and fight her way out, with her blaster if need be.

Then she heard a voice call out.

Chapter 15

"Halt!"

Liberty looked wildly out into the vast garden. A Redcoat pointed at her. Others followed his direction.

"You there!"

Liberty didn't answer. She was crouched by the window, willing to fight for her love. But she knew her only option was to escape. She would be no help if she was caught. She dashed through the garden, between two armed soldiers. They and two others chased her into the woods.

Liberty followed the rising moon. A shadow eclipsed the bright orb. She paused, acclimating her eyes to the variance in dark and light. The shadow moved. It appeared as a great bird. It was coming from the South, from Boston proper.

"There she is!" The call sent a shiver of adrenaline through Liberty's body. She looked towards the clearing before her and fled.

Desperately, she bounded into the clearing. It wasn't easy to run in her heavy apron.

Ahead of her, she saw the glint of weapons. She was surrounded! She froze, unwilling to surrender without a fight, but not seeing any other options. A shadow crossed her face again. She looked up.

A giant golden rooster hovered above. It was stunning, gleaming in the full moon. Across its broad chest she could read the words: *SCEPTRE DE AJAX*.

Could it be? The French?

A rope dropped from a compartment in the mechanical creature's belly. Liberty leapt and climbed, while the Redcoats stared, dumbfounded.

Liberty didn't know where she was going, but the unknown was a better alternative to a fate of hanging for treason.

She climbed the rope, and as she did, it was pulled up with a great mechanical pulley system. The Redcoats broke their stupor and ran forward, but they were too late. Liberty approached the dark gut of the monstrous fowl. A hand reached down. She grabbed it and was hoisted into the belly of the beast.

Crumpled across a gleaming wood floor outlaid with gold leaf, Liberty tried to get her bearings. She pushed herself up to a squat. Her heart battered her chest with exertion and anxiety. The same hand that had grabbed hers was before her, offering a crystal glass full of a clear liquid with bubbling fizz.

Liberty had never seen anything like it. She looked up and met the eyes of her savior. Her quick breath hitched as she became instantly alert.

The man wore a foreign uniform trimmed with gold brocade tracing the trail of shining brass buttons of the black waistcoat, with a white neckcloth over his white shirt. White silk pants with red and blue stripes running vertically along long legs were belted with a flowy red scarf.

His concerned face was distinctive, with a long nose and dainty lips. His dark brown tousled hair gave him a look of ready mischief. When his deep brown eyes met hers, she was almost sure of her assessment, but not enough to trust, even though this man had ultimately saved her from immediate violence.

"Please, partake of this drink, and rejuvenate." The thick, luscious accent. It had to be.

"Pardon me, but whose presence am I in?" Liberty accepted the crystal glass with the bubbling liquid but did not drink it, even though her parched body cried out for satiation.

The man stood, stretching to his full grand height. He looked surprised. "Forgive me for not introducing myself. It is I, le Marquis de Lafayette." His jowled chin stuck out in pride.

Liberty's eyes widened. Georgia was never going to believe this. At the thought of her captured lover, fresh fire flowed through her heart. She took a gulp of the liquid and started coughing.

"What is this?"

"Why, champagne of course!" Liberty had no idea what that was exactly, but her dry throat thanked her.

LaFayette waited for her expectantly.

Liberty decided to lay it all on the line. "You may call me Liberty. You saved me, and I thank you, from bloodthirsty Redcoats. They were chasing me from an insurrection at Governor Hutchinson's mansion and they have the lady of the house, his daughter, captive. I attempted to save her... and failed."

LaFayette's smooth voice covered her with a benign sense of calm. "The battle has not yet begun. You will save her yet."

"Battle?"

Lafayette's deep eyes bore into hers with fierce determination. "You seem to be brave and strong, a true ally against the vindictive British. Fly with me, with us, to Boston Harbor, where we will arrive and show them the strength of allies."

"And the power when resistance meets persistence." Liberty stood and wobbled a bit.

"Do not worry. You will get your sky legs soon enough. Now," he motioned for Liberty to follow him, "we fly!"

Liberty chose to trust this charming and action-oriented legend. Lafayette led her to a galley where massive control panels lined the walls.

Through windows in the neck of the giant flying rooster, Liberty helped Lafayette navigate around the edge of the woods.

"What is the plan?"

Lafayette kept his eyes on the glass shields. "We have allies waiting for us. The plan is to attack the harbor. But I have it on good word that the British have sent a fleet of waterships filled with reinforcements and a cache of weapons."

"That was me, that was my word!"

"I do not question that."

Lafayette glanced at her and took in her disheveled appearance. "I recognize the odor of smoke on you. Are you well?"

Liberty squared her shoulders. "Well enough to fight back!" She was alert now with the idea of battle ahead of her. "The Redcoats were to come at the rising of the moon—and that is now! We must attack them before they make it to shore!"

"We will. And we'll do it with style."

Liberty stared out the windows. “There, beyond those pines, the landscape lowers and soon we will be over the harbor. If we can get there before the Redcoat waterships do, we can block the entrance to the harbor.”

“That is the plan.”

Liberty pointed into the night. “There! To the right!! I see lights!”

“I do believe that is the British waterships we have been seeking.”

“But that means we’re too late!” Liberty was anguished. Was all her suffering for naught? Was she fated to never see her beloved Georgia again?

“Not too late. Just time to re-evaluate.”

Liberty considered this for a moment. She took a deep breath and started coughing again. Her insides still burned with the breath of fire. “We could head out and circumvent the harbor, then come around to block them in. Hopefully the Patriots can get there soon enough to keep them at bay before they land.”

“*Bon*. And if our allies support us, as I believe them to be already be in place for, this should be a hell of a fight, and an enormous victory.”

Liberty looked across the moonlit sea. “Just don’t sail too far past the dark waters.”

Lafayette nodded. “I hear you.”

"Truly, please take heed. We must remain as close to shore as possible. The dark waters must be avoided."

Lafayette looked at her sidelong as he pedaled, maintaining motion on the mecha-bird's wings. "Afraid of drowning?"

"Something like that. Just please, be cautious."

Lafayette briefly smiled. "I will. Although I prefer to throw caution to the wind."

Chapter 16

They reached the open water and circled back so they were behind the fleet of three British waterships.

"Perfect timing, Liberty! To the trebuchet!" Lafayette dismounted the pedals. Liberty followed him up a flight of narrow stairs to a cache of shallow barrels. Lafayette unscrewed the tops and rolled them out of the way. "Load the trebuchet!"

"Where?" asked Liberty, but it seemed Lafayette couldn't hear her over the grinding of gears. Something on the landing unfolded. The rooster's beak had opened. She could see through to the moon shining over the mouth of the harbor. Tall white masts of the British sky ships billowed in the wind power provided by forced hot air. Cold Atlantic water was siphoned into a big black cauldron, creating steam. This steam rose and was diverted through the massive lion-shaped cover. The statue's roar was a blast of steam, allowing the direction of the ships to be diverted.

Liberty saw a cannon being loaded and aimed upward. “Incoming!”

“If we act quickly, we can avoid it!” Lafayette lifted the barrels and gently sifted their contents into a trebuchet he had rolled out of the rooster’s tongue.

Liberty joined him. She investigated a barrel. “Are those, couldn’t be, croissants?”

Lafayette’s small mouth opened to a proud grin. “Explosives!”

The trebuchet was launched, croissants zipped through the air, and exploded upon impact, striking the water and not much else.

“Again!”

Liberty loaded the trebuchet. This time the croissants filled a watership’s deck with black fiery holes. Lafayette let out a cry of victory.

The two remaining waterships turned opposite ways, one towards the giant rooster and one towards the shore.

“Quick!” shouted Liberty. “Before they aim their cannons at innocent colonists!”

Lafayette launched the next load of croissants upon the British watership below them.

“The mast is damaged, and look! We have destroyed a cannon!”

"*Bien tot.*" Lafayette was in his realm, in the heat of battle.

Liberty felt a sense of jubilation. Maybe the odds were not against her after all. She helped launch the trebuchet again. The water below them splashed with wayward explosives, but many hit their mark again. Another watership began to sink.

The excitement in the cockpit quickly subdued when the pair saw the third watership floating dangerously close to the harbor.

Great round forms breeched and bobbed in the water, roughened by battle.

"What are those?" Liberty could not believe her eyes. "They look like giant turtles!"

"Indeed!" Lafayette leaned over the empty trebuchet. Both he and Liberty were sweating profusely. "La Tortuga Armada! The Spanish have been lying in wait for this moment!"

The shell of a turtle opened on massive hinges. From inside, Spanish militia lit a fuse, and a missile rose from the shell and torpedoed into the water. The last watership maintained its delicate distance between the armada and the skyship. It fired back, destroying the turtle submersible, but others bobbed and unhinged in the roiling water.

"We have them surrounded!" Liberty exclaimed.

Lafayette reloaded the trebuchet. "This last bundle should stop them."

Liberty's eyes searched the water for the next best place to aim.

But what was that?

In the moonlight, she watched in horror as long tentacles with fingered tendrils at the ends rose from the harbor. All the warnings she had ever heard about the dark sea blasted in her head.

She could hear the Redcoats scream below. "'Tis the Kraken!"

But Liberty knew better. This was not a mere sea monster. It was a terror of the deep.

Mountainous legs covered in barnacles rose as the horrifying entity stood. Its feet suckled at the mud where two worlds met.

The gigantic being's head sprouted with tentacles. One central eye stared unblinking at the rooster. It reached one arm out and grasped at it, but quick-thinking Lafayette jumped onto the pedals to spin backwards. "Liberty! The trebuchet!"

She launched the last of the croissants from the trebuchet. They hit the one-eyed thing in its wide stomach. A groan of anguish emanated like thunder. The creature stumbled back.

The last watership bombed its back. The massive monster fell to its knees.

Then the armada's torpedoes skimmed the water and knocked into the gruesome giant. It caught itself with a mighty thump of its fists on the rocky harbor floor.

It rose again, stomping on the armada as it did so, sinking several turtles. The watership continued bombarding it with cannonballs.

"We are out of ammunition!" cried Liberty. Her life flashed before her eyes. Her beloved Georgia. Her print shop. Her ink.

"We can attack with our sharp beak! If we die, we die for glory!"

"I'd rather live for freedom!"

The treacherous beast had risen again. Its long tentacles squirmed through the air. They stretched out to the skyship.

"Look out!"

Lafayette reached up to pull the ropes that enacted the wing's mechanisms. It rose. But Lafayette had misjudged the distance.

The tentacles stretched from the head to entangle the skyship. Lafayette fell from the pedals and held onto the ropes, his feet dangling in the cockpit.

Liberty could still hear the pounding and blasting sounds of the Spanish and British fighting against the monster. Nothing seemed able to stop it. And now she was bracing herself against a wall, staring into the anomaly's one huge yellow eye with a rectangular pupil. It stared back.

She thought again of all she loved, and all she would never love again. Without Georgia, and her print shop, and a hope for true freedom, she had nothing. She held her right hand to her heart, as if she could stop the grief from pouring out.

Something poked through her apron into the palm of her hand. In her misery, she almost didn't feel it. But still it pressed in, sharper as her sorrow deepened. Then the small pain brought her to a fresh consciousness.

She knew what was in her pocket.

The one thing she always counted on.

She pulled out her precious copper quill. This was her last hope.

Her knees bent as she steadied herself. She removed the long ribbon from her hair. She clenched her molars down on one end, and with her left hand, pulled it taut. Then she positioned the quill's copper feathers on the ribbon and pulled back. She aimed. She knew this was her last chance for any possibility of life.

The one eye of the abyss.

She released the quill and it shot out into the moonlight, like a blazing flash.

The giant eye was pierced deep by Revere's copper, and the Old One fell.

The tentacles released the skyship in writhing agony. With the sound of a sucking void, the dreadful giant's remains sank into the shallow depths of the Boston Harbor.

Liberty clung to a wayward spring. Lafayette swung into the stirrups and desperately pulled at the wing ropes.

The frothy bubbles in the water rose and popped at the surface. The monster was dead.

Her joy was rattled when she remembered that there was still battle ahead.

But for just a moment, it was good to be alive.

Chapter 17

Liberty and Lafayette effectively righted the giant cock. Liberty gazed through its mouth.

Below her was a rancid mess. Fish flipped dead at the curves of the harbor. The water deepened to a darker black than her ink.

But there was silence.

No cannonballs.

No torpedoes.

No exploding croissants.

"Lafayette," she called, then lowered her voice. It sounded hollow in the deathly pungent stink of monster flesh. A whisper was loud enough. "Listen!"

"I do not hear anything."

"My point! The battle has stopped! That can mean only one thing! A ceasefire. Imagine! We were here to fight the British and witness the birth of a new country! We were here when the British Empire surrendered to freedom!"

Lafayette looked from the trebuchet to Liberty. "We are out of ammunition."

"What?"

"*Je suis a court de munitions.*"

Liberty looked out across the harbor. Rowboats and canoes retrieved the Redcoats from the bow of the sinking ship. The turtles paddled onto a sandbar.

Her armistice was simply a lack of weaponry and ammunition.

But she knew who had weapons. And just who the British would be after next. The Minutemen!

Lafayette nodded, already thinking ahead like she was. "The British will storm the countryside and gain control there. They could just burn each town as they race through."

"I wouldn't put it past them."

"Someone has to warn them!" Lafayette raised his goggles, taming back his wind-whipped locks.

"I will warn them. I will shout it for all to hear. Then each person can choose to fight the brutality of tyranny."

"Yet, how, Liberty?"

"Look below!"

Lafayette eyed her with concern. "You plan on swimming?"

"No! Even better!"

"I don't see anything, but I hear a quacking sound."

Liberty was already lowering the rope. "I'll send help for you too!"

"Do not worry. I will find my own way out, I always do."

Liberty shook his hand. "Anyway, why did you save me in the first place?"

"Because any enemy of Great Britain is a friend of mine."

Liberty shimmied down the rope to the quacking automaton. She spread her legs and clutched at the feathers sewn into the fabric that covered the barrel encasing the mechanisms. She closed her eyes until the nausea passed. The smell of the enormous creature's carcass was like pig entrails infested by maggots. There was no escape from the odor. She set the coordinates for the trail of the Charles River.

The duck's gears shifted. Liberty spun the handles stuck through each side of the automaton's throat. Its mouth opened and an accordion announced itself with a duck call. Liberty reached into its open mouth and pulled out the quacker. She was hatching a plan, and needed a sense of quiet to make it come to fruition.

Liberty breathed out deeply as she lay across the paddling duck's back. The duckboat had been built as a tugboat, but must have become freed from dock in the melee. After a few minutes to get her bearings, Liberty changed the coordinates in the pegs of the automaton's setup. She slid off into the mud and realized that she had lost her shoes along the way. Then she shipped the duck off to Boston. Maybe it would find Lafayette eventually.

Then, in stocking feet, she ran through the night to the next town. The cold wet earth sucked at her feet as she rushed to spread the word.

She slammed her fists into the first door she came to. Christ Church. "The Regulars are coming out! The Regulars are coming out!"

She heard the doors unlatch from inside. The door opened a crack, and the startled sexton stared wide-eyed at the wild-looking woman before him.

"Are you in need of help?" he asked, holding a candelabra in one hand, and the other hand still on the door knob.

"Yes, we must alert everyone that the Regulars are out and bringing war this way."

"The church will be a place of asylum. We have blankets and a food store here."

"Ring the church bell to summon the parish. Then you can provide safety for the women and children, while the men fight."

"And you?" The sexton looked unsure.

"I will continue to spread the word.

Liberty took off into the night. She had just passed a familiar grove when she heard the church bell toll.

Aware of her aloneness, she wondered about Georgia. If only she could simply climb up to her window and see her, and hold her, feel her soft hair, tell her she loved her. Again and again.

She couldn't go through the countryside warning strangers when her own beloved was being held hostage! Now might be her only chance to save her!

She followed the ridge of the woods to the Governor's Manson and hid in a thicket. Something shuffled in the dead leaves. Liberty froze. The shuffle came again, then silence. Liberty caught movement out of the corner of her eye. Just a rabbit. She wasn't afraid of the harmless animal. But she was wary of what preyed upon it.

She looked across the rocky glade towards the estate. There was a small bonfire in front of the mansion. In the flickering shadows that reflected off of the mansion's windows, she saw no one. She crept up closer and raced towards the shrubbery. From there she could see that the bonfire was circled by empty stools. Where had the redcoats gone?

Liberty crawled beneath the bushes and slunk around the mansion's corners to the back. She looked up at Georgia's window and saw a faint glow.

She climbed up the tree, skinning her ankles in the process. She peeked in the window.

There was Georgia! Alone in her room, frantically shoving rolled up skirts and shirts into a large knapsack.

Liberty scratched at the window. Georgia startled, then saw her beloved beyond the glass. She threw the window open.

Liberty came tumbling in. "Georgia! Are you alright?"

"Yes, now that you're here!"

The two women embraced and their tears mixed together.

"I am so, so sorry I left you. I didn't want to."

"I know, I was so worried about you! I didn't know what happened to you."

"Did they hurt you?" asked Liberty.

"They were quite rough but they didn't hurt me. They boarded up Father's secret escape hatch and locked me in here. I still do not know what has become of Father. I heard an outcry and tumult, something about a giant cock, and knew something was going foul. I decided to pack up some clothes and be ready for the next step, whatever that would be."

"The next step, is ours, together. War is coming from the sea. You and I can race over to Christ Church. The sexton is accepting refugees. You could go there and help with the women and children while the men go to fight."

"Where does that leave you?" Georgia's eyes were full of tears.

"There has to be a way to spread the word about the redcoats approaching, and I am it, until at least someone else can take up the call in my place."

"I was afraid of something like that."

"We can be brave together. Let's start by finding a way out. I can help you climb out the window and down the tree. Then we can run for it!"

"The window? Liberty, I don't think I can do that."

"I'll help you."

Georgia pulled up her skirts and leaned against the windowsill. She looked down at the cold ground.

"I just do not think I can physically do it."

Liberty started to sweat. Her mind clouded over with anxiety. She took a deep breath and blew out hard. She knew she needed to think clearly in order to survive.

Both Liberty and Georgia stared at the door.

"I don't hear any movement from the rest of the mansion, do you?"

Georgia shook her head.

"I have a feeling that the redcoats were alerted to the battle and hurried to leave. It's possible that they have all gone. It is also possible that some have remained to secure the estate. But if we assume the mansion has been evacuated, then we could try to break out of this room without being noticed."

"It seems like the best shot we have," agreed Georgia. "I just hope that Father is safe."

"Before we can ensure his safety, we need to ensure yours. Otherwise how will you be able to aid him if he needs it?"

"You're right. Let's get out of here."

Liberty knelt and peered through the keyhole of Georgia's bedroom door. There were no shadows cast by the lit sconces on the landing. No draft of breath or movement flickered the flames. Now to figure out how to unlock the door.

She stood, and with her left hand pressed on the door jam, and with her right hand she grasped the doorknob. She wanted to test out the weight of the door. Maybe she and Georgia could find a way to pull the door open using tied sheets. Or maybe—

Liberty stumbled backwards, knocking into Georgia.

"It was unlocked!" shouted Liberty in triumphant surprise.

"Some soldier with a genteel heart must have done me a last good turn. I hope Father was proffered equal mercy."

Liberty stood in the doorway and peered out into the hallway leading to the staircase.

"I've got my knapsack. I am ready for what awaits us."

Liberty stood still, one foot in the bedroom, one foot in the hallway.

“What is it?”

“I just never thought, in all these years, that this would be the way I pass through your front door.”

“It all seems so silly now, doesn’t it? I just want to be with you, Liberty, and to help keep the peace in our colony. Two simple things. Nothing else matters to me right now.”

“Let us make it so.”

Liberty followed Georgia down the stairs, slowly as each floorboard creaked. They made it to the front door.

“They really have abandoned the mansion after all. Lucky for us!” Liberty and Georgia crept into the thicket. “Do you think you can find your way to Christ Church from here?”

“Yes, I do.”

“Then you know what to do.”

“Oh, Liberty, I feel like I just got you back, and now I’ve got to let you go again! This is killing me!”

Liberty pulled her into her arms. “We will be together again.”

“I’ll go up to the tower and light a lantern for you, to guide your heart back to me.”

“Light one for yourself, too, so our lights can shine together.”

"Liberty, I love you."

"I love you."

"Now, let's go!"

The two women sprang from the thicket, each running in different directions, hoping that their final destination would be together.

Liberty continued shouting until she reached the outskirts of the countryside of Waltham. It hurt to yell, and her voice was almost gone. Her sides ached from exertion. She couldn't feel her frozen feet. Finally, she gave in to rest.

She found it odd how quiet the night was. It had the normal night sounds of spring peepers and owls, coyotes on the hunt—and that was the problem. This was no ordinary night. Where were the Patriots? Why hadn't the Patriots in Boston sent out a call of warning to the countryside? Why was the world at peace when a war was waging?

Then she heard a whinny, although she was not near any homes. Just a small town corner, with no lights in empty doorways. The unmistakable sound of a horse neighing. Something else too, high and pretty, like a song.

She got up to investigate.

A hefty brown flesh horse was kicking at the crossing gate. The rider hadn't enacted the switch to swing the door open. But where was the rider?

Then she saw a tricorn hat by the horse's hind hooves. And a crumpled body in the brown beauty's shadow.

Liberty cautiously approached the horse. And the rider, whose face she could now see, shining in the dark in a frozen jolly smile. The dented copper face was difficult to place, but the stocky build and attire were instantly recognizable.

"Mr. Revere!"

Behind the smiling lips a tinny voice repeated, "The Regulars are coming out! The Regulars are coming out!" The soundbox in the decapitated hero's throat spun on.

Liberty cradled the machine's head in her hands. "No wonder there is no outcry in the streets! No wonder nobody has collected to fight! Nobody knows!"

She laid Mr. Revere's detached head down at its spot on the ground above the neck. She looked at the flesh horse and ascertained what had happened. The horse had been running at full speed when it was stopped abruptly by the closed gate, causing the automaton to lurch forward and off its back. With no one to open the gate, it waited.

Liberty addressed the horse.

"Hello, brown beauty. Could you take me through the countryside? We have got to warn the others and assemble the

Minutemen. It looks like you and I are going to have to team up, and I've never ridden a horse. But I've seen plenty of people doing it." She touched the side of the massive flesh beast's body, and the horse nuzzled her gently, which was frightening.

"Glad that's settled. One more thing." She leaned down and retrieved the tricorn hat from the ground. "I hope you don't mind, Mr. Revere, but I will take the call from here. Perhaps wearing your hat will give me credence." She dusted it off with her hands and turned the gear on the red, white and blue cockade on the hat. She placed it on her head and turned back to the horse, taking a deep breath. Her head swam with all she had encountered and lived through this day. She thought about Georgia, a refugee. She had to save her. And the only way she could do that was to save Massachusetts. Tonight.

She awkwardly mounted the horse and pressed the button to open the door. She slapped the reins, and encouraged, "C'mon, girl!" The horse sprang into action, and Liberty carried the call.

Chapter 18

Liberty had never ridden a flesh horse before. She lost hold of the reins and clung to the horse's neck as she lay along the back of the animal, the ridges of the saddle barely keeping her in place.

She pushed her way up and regained control of the reins. The last row of shops passed in a blur, but not before Liberty screeched her loudest. She came to a publick house and guided Brown Beauty closer. She dismounted and dashed through the doors.

"Patriots! Gather! War is upon us! The British are coming, and we must prepare for battle!"

A great roar rose up from the masculine voices. She made her way to the bar. "I need weak drink for a strong voice." The barkeep looked at her soot-covered clothes, and the oversized tricorn hat on her head.

"At once!" He poured her a drink which she swallowed in three gulps. "Help yourself to whatever you need." The bartender removed his apron, lifted a musket from behind the bar, and charged out.

Liberty returned to the horse, helping herself to a trough of water. "That's it, girl. Now we must ride again." She balanced on the trough to make it easier for her to climb onto the horse's back.

At twilight, Liberty reached Lexington. The entire countryside had heeded Liberty's warning. She dismounted Brown Beauty and joined the fray. Orders were being shouted and obeyed, and with quick intensity, a contingent of trained Minutemen stood in a human barricade before the other colonial Patriots. Boys with fifes and drums played uproarious battle songs.

At sunrise, the British troops found what they had been looking for. The mass of Patriots stood firm, weaponry loaded and at the ready. The British laughed at them and their crude artillery. With the Crown's sophisticated fighting tools, the British were sure of a dignified win.

Liberty joined the ferment with fierceness. She wiggled her way between mechanical wolves with jagged teeth, huge beavers with crushing tails, and piles of grass-woven rabbits filled with explosive pellets, ready to be launched into enemy lines. She saw Knox with his two mecha-oxen pulling canons into the battle line. Her cracked feet did not slow her progress.

She stood at the ready among the Minutemen.

A British colonel shouted through his voice cone. "In the name of King George III, I order you to lay down your weapons and disband!"

Liberty's heart pounded for battle, even though her heart desired peace. Peace for Georgia. Peace for the colonies.

Native people from tribes throughout the colony joined the fight with the Patriots. Liberty looked across the front line and saw Native people geared up at the British lines as well. Liberty shook her head. "The Redcoats will never give them leniency. They have chosen the wrong side to fight for."

Liberty's eyes scanned the army. Then she saw him. And he saw her. Lieutenant Burch. He plucked her blood and ink-stained glove from his belt and waved it in the air. Then he pulled up his rifle and aimed.

"Hold your fire!" The British colonel was steadfast in his warning as he patrolled the gathered army.

Farm boys shook as they looked at each other for guidance.

Liberty was deadly focused. She had never felt so calm, yet so alert, in all of her life.

Across the way, she watched the Redcoats hesitate with their weapons at the ready. She saw Burch in the crowd, and their eyes met.

"One last time! Lower your weapons!"

All was quiet. Even the fifes and drums had stopped playing, and the air no longer echoed with the clomp of British boots.

Liberty knew what she was doing, what she was about to do, and that her next move could change her, and perhaps the world.

She pulled her air blaster from deep in her lowest apron pocket. She gripped it with both hands. She lined it up with careful aim.

And pulled the trigger.

Epilogue

Georgia finished her vegetable gardening and read the latest news posted on a tree outside her new humble home, from the *Patriot Herald.*

"King George III declares armistice. There will be peace in the colonies that remain, except for New England. Colonists in New England are to be outcast from the rest of the continent. All who stay will never leave. All Massachusetts inhabitants are thus offered the option to flee to British territories. Thirty days grace. After that, those who persist in living in New England will be considered outcasts and a Great Wall shall be built by the Native people to enclose these rebels to the ocean. With the growing technology of sky ships, Britain will soon possess ample power to transport heavy cargo. Keep your out-of-date watership ports. Enjoy eating cod."

Georgia entered her new large, but rather plain, abode. She set her gardening implements in a tin bucket by the door and wiped her hands down her brown apron. The whirr of spinning rolls and the smell of ink welcomed her.

It had been fourteen months since the Battle at Lexington and Concord. An unsteady peace was now secured. Georgia walked through the foyer where chairs were set up for the next meeting of the Americans. She entered the back room, cavernous and deep. Large windows let in the bright, fresh sunlight.

Hunched over, now with more silver than red in her hair, Liberty looked up and smiled. “How are you, my love?” She stepped away from the refurbished printing press to bring Georgia a tender kiss.

“I am ordinary in every way, but you, Liberty, are extraordinary.”

“You, my dear, are exquisite. The country will never forget your grace and strength, and your donations of resources to the building of our new nation. The way you turned the mansion into a hospital, for both sides, is admirable beyond compare.” Liberty hammered the final rivet into her new invention. A metal sheet slid over the press. “The truth must be protected.”

She took off her apron and extended her arm to Georgia. They left the printing press and closed the door behind them.

“I received a letter today from Father. His exile is surprisingly a welcome change from the rigors of government.

He is enjoying tropical breezes and long walks on sandy shores with crystal clear waters."

"I know you miss him."

"I do. Yet, I would not give up my life with you for anything."

"I indeed would not trade this life for anything."

"Even freedom?" Georgia teased.

"This is freedom."

Liberty and Georgia paused to join hands and look into each other's eyes.

"And remember," said Liberty, her chest swelling with hope and confidence. "It all begins with the freedom to love."

The bell above the front door rang. Henry Knox stepped in.

"Liberty, I was given another sheepskin to print, along with a hefty sum to deliver it to you. And I have brought you hemp parchment, as well."

Liberty unrolled the scroll. Her eyes widened, and tears escaped her eyes.

"Are you alright?" asked Knox.

Georgia wrapped an arm around Liberty's shoulders and peered at the thick words.

Liberty smiled, her eyes shining. "A Declaration from Congress! Freedom has been established! We are officially no longer under British rule!"

Georgia enveloped Liberty in a hug.

"Triumph!" said Knox.

"Freedom," murmured Liberty.

Beyond the print shop, past the woods, in the Boston Harbor, the giant's body rotted by the shore. The stench caused widespread retching, and the slimy carcass attracted disease. Rankness poisoned the water and the land as it decomposed. The British and Loyalists were relieved to leave the corpse and flee back to Great Britain.

The Native people were awarded this territory because neither the Crown nor the new country particularly wanted it.

The Great One slept in death while from its bones a new way of life began.

Bravery, tenacity, hope, and community. From all of that came freedom. But it all began with love.

###

Acknowledgements

Rivets and Revolution has been my passion for ten months, and I have so many people to thank for feeding that flame.

To my faithful readers, I appreciate your support throughout the creation of this book. Thank you for every word or act of encouragement.

I would like to acknowledge my K.S. campaign backers who generously and with faith invested in me. Family, friends, readers, steampunks, the wildly adventurous, you all came together to financially support this book, and I am grateful.

A special thank you to Douglas Yeager, true champion of the arts, for all of your support—and thank you for reminding me of how fabulous the French can be!

Our cover designer, Steven Novak Illustrations, created this cover and captured the spirit of Liberty. This is his eighth cover he made exclusively for me.

With deepest thanks and gratitude to my exemplary editor, Gevera Bert Piedmont, who fine-tuned this story above and beyond my greatest expectations. There is no one else I have so trusted with my writing. Without you, Bert, where would Georgia be?

With gratitude to the museums and organizations that proved to be excellent resources throughout my research. The Waltham Museum and The Waltham Historical Society, especially. Also including The Museum of Printing, Old

Sturbridge Village, the Peabody Essex Museum, Lexington Visitors Center, the Charles River Museum of Industry and Innovation, and Historic New England. And special hugs to everyone at the Waltham Arts Council for cheering me on!

Thank you to my dear Peter Payack, for guiding me to local historic sites and exploring the concepts of how climate and weather affected the American Revolution. From Boston to Salem, every excursion an adventure. Your empathy, your uplifting viewpoints when I made a major technical mistake, and your dependable friendship walked with me throughout. Next Mike's Pastry is on me. I love you.

Thank you friend and fellow author Ashley Grant. It was exciting to write our latest books at the same time!

In honor of those who fought for freedom from tyranny during the Revolutionary War, including my own ancestors. During 2025, particularly, as we commemorate the 250th anniversary of the shot heard round the world, let us strengthen and grow together.

About the Author

Jessica Lucci is a poet and steampunk author who writes about modern issues while maintaining historic integrity. All of her books feature multi-faceted LGBTQ+ main characters. She makes her home in Waltham, Massachusetts, U.S.A., where she serves as president of the Waltham Arts Council, on the board of directors for the Waltham Museum and Waltham Pride Fest.

She was a featured artist for her poetry at Watch City Arts, May, 2023. Her haiku was included in an installation commemorating the 20th anniversary of the Minuteman Bikeway. Her haiku has also been installed in Arlington and Lexington, and her poetry was included in the "Moody Street Art Walk." Her works include the steampunk "Watch City" trilogy, and *Salem Switch*; and the poetry collections *How Can I Steal a Purse* and *Graveyard Shift*. When not writing and reading, she time travels at steampunk festivals and Renaissance faires.

This is your page, dear reader, to write in as you wish.

www.ingramcontent.com/pod-product-compliance
Lightning Source LLC
Chambersburg PA
CBHW070309280626
47159CB00018B/3332
* 9 7 8 1 7 3 2 3 4 9 5 7 5 *